Thoroughly Modern Amanda

by

Susan Macatee

This is a work of fiction. Names, characters, places, and incidents are either the product of the author's imagination or are used fictitiously, and any resemblance to actual persons living or dead, business establishments, events, or locales, is entirely coincidental.

Thoroughly Modern Amanda

Cover Art by *Debbie Taylor*

The Wild Rose Press, Inc.
PO Box 708
Adams Basin, NY 14410-0708
Visit us at www.thewildrosepress.com

Publishing History
First American Rose Edition, 2012
Digital ISBN 978-1-61217-586-7
Print ISBN 978-1-62830-157-1

Published in the United States of America

She led Jack to one of the chairs by the staircase. "Sit here a minute. I'll open the parlor doors so you can lie on the settee, then I'll find my stepmother."

He sat with a thump, his tanned, work-roughened hand reaching for his head.

"Does it still hurt?" she asked.

He nodded. "A little. You have any ibuprofen by any chance?"

She frowned. "Ibu…I'm not sure what you mean."

He heaved a heavy sigh and sank his face into both hands.

"Just a minute. I'll get you into the parlor."

She flung open the doors and found the parlor empty, as she'd expected. The room was hardly used, except for those rare occasions when a family member entertained guests. But Mrs. O'Leary had cleaned the small room yesterday, so there shouldn't be any dust. She ran her hand over the settee by the fireplace to be sure.

Turning back to the hall, she strode over to Jack. He peered up at her, his eyes bleary. She lifted her hand, and he settled his over hers. His firm, strong grip sent a tingle through her fingers. What would it feel like to have those hands roving over her body? Her face heated at the thought.

Praise for Susan Macatee

ERIN'S REBEL
Finalist, Ancient City Romance Authors
2010 Reader's Choice Award, paranormal category
"I love historical romances and Susan Macatee did a beautiful job with this one."
~Night Owl Reviews (4.5 Hearts)
"I loved the author's gentle hand with detail, her convincing touch with romance, and the twists and turns that she creates before a thoroughly satisfying ending...This book's well worth keeping on my shelf."
~WRDF Reviews
"Recommended read for paranormal and historical romance readers or if you simply enjoy a good love story."
~ParaNormal Romance
"*ERIN'S REBEL* is rich in history and mystery."
~TwoLips Reviews (4 Lips)

~~*~~

CONFEDERATE ROSE
1st place, First Coast Romance Writers
2010 Beacon Contest for Published Authors, historical category
2nd place, 2010 New England Reader's
Choice Bean Pot Award, historical category
"If you like romance wrapped in the conflicts of the Civil War you will definitely enjoy this book."
~You Gotta Read Reviews
"*CONFEDERATE ROSE* is a magnificent work of fiction...I highly recommend this charming historical."
~Blue Ribbon Reviews at Romance Junkies

Dedication

To my new granddaughter, Arabella. May your imagination soar as you grow and always stay as sweet as you are now.
And to my husband...always encouraging and proud, even if he doesn't completely understand my compulsion to write.

Chapter One

Carver, Pennsylvania
April 4, 1881

Amanda Montgomery paced the main office of *The Carver Weekly.* For the past three months, she'd held a position of feature writer and office assistant at the small town newspaper.

Stepping toward the supervising editor's office, she scowled through the glass-topped door at the massive mahogany desk where Mr. Randolph Norwood worked. Pushing the door open, she slipped inside, her heels clicking against the polished floor. She propped her hands on her hips and scanned the empty room.

Ten minutes before, his secretary had left a message that Randolph summoned her to discuss her latest assignment. She'd told the woman she'd be there as soon as possible but needed to complete the finishing touches on her last assignment. And now she was here; Randolph wasn't.

Twice this week, she'd caught him flirting with his secretary, Miss Carson, a buxom dark-haired beauty. Randolph assured Amanda the exchange was entirely innocent. He considered the woman an excellent secretary and nothing more.

Amanda pulled the door closed. Her heavy skirts swished along the hardwood floor as she paced, her eye on the office door.

I should just leave and allow him to wonder where I am.

She stepped toward the door, her hand outstretched, but thought better of it. If she wasn't here when he arrived, he might accuse her of slacking and send her home.

She'd first met Randolph at the home of one of her father's associates during a dinner party. His stories of working as a supervising editor for the weekly paper intrigued her. Even as a child, she'd dreamed of being a writer, like her stepmother.

After learning of her interest, Randolph offered her a job as a reporter on the condition she allow him to court her. He was handsome and attentive, and she'd accepted his offer on the spot, excited to have an actual job outside of the home. Her father actually approved, believing Randolph a desirable suitor for his only daughter, although her stepmother had reservations about the man's intentions.

Amanda slid her hand over the smooth desktop, wondering how it would feel to be a supervisor in charge of writers. If she were giving out the assignments, she wouldn't relegate the women writers to fluff features of women's groups and church socials. She'd make sure everyone who worked here had an equal chance. Her stepmother always told her, though men and women had their differences, both sexes had the same capabilities and talents.

She eyed the closed door again. Lifting her chin, she stepped around the desk, pulled out the chair, and settled into it. With an audible sigh of pleasure, she leaned back and surveyed the papers on the desk surface. A pad caught her eye. Leaning forward, she squinted to make out the scrawled handwriting—*Miss Montgomery, interview Mrs. Grenshaw about the items needed for the Carver church social bake sale this coming Sunday.*

She grasped the pad.

How dare he? He'd promised her an interview with the newly elected councilman, Mr. Ernest Pryor.

Her face heated in humiliation. He'd all but sworn the meaty assignment was hers.

The door creaked. She dropped the pad and rose from the chair, smoothing her skirts. Miss Carson's heart shaped face appeared, her dark brows lifting.

"Oh, I'm sorry, Miss Montgomery!" She stepped into the office, a stack of papers in her arms. "Mr. Norwood was delayed. He'll be along soon."

Amanda nodded. "Should I leave and come back?"

Miss Carson shook her head, sending her carefully arranged bun bobbing. "Oh, no. You can wait here. I'll tell him I let you in."

Amanda shrugged. "I guess I'll have a seat then." She settled back in Norwood's chair.

Miss Carson's lips pursed, but she nodded. "I'll be just outside and alert Mr. Norwood when he returns."

After the secretary closed the door, Amanda grinned.

She occupied her time sifting through the papers layered on Norwood's desk. Catching sight of the assignment he'd promised her, she noted Glen Bradshaw's name on the top of the sheet.

The weasel. Bradshaw had joined the paper's staff two weeks ago and already had his eyes on Amanda's job. No wonder she'd been relegated to the church social assignment. When Randolph returned, she'd have it out with him. He couldn't make promises and break them just because she was a woman.

She propped her elbow on the desk and rested her chin in her hand. Deep in thought, she glanced up when the door opened and Norwood strode into the room.

His brow furrowed. Apparently Miss Carson had warned him of Amanda's presence.

"I'm terribly sorry, Amanda." He hastened around the desk to her side, reaching for her hand. "I was held up."

Amanda didn't rise but slid the chair back, shifting beyond his reach. She tapped her fingertips on the desk top. "So I surmised."

"If you would please?" His lips thinned to a straight line beneath his thin mustache, as he motioned to his chair.

"Oh, of course." Amanda held her lips firm in an effort not to break out in a broad smile.

He adjusted his tie and motioned to the chair opposite his desk as he settled into his seat.

She lifted her skirts, catching his downward gaze. He obviously hoped to catch a glimpse of her ankles. She sat and arranged her skirts so she was decently covered, trying to suppress a laugh.

After biting her lip, she leaned forward. "What did you want to see me about?"

He shuffled papers, the tick in his cheek working. "I was forced to change your assignment."

"Oh?" Amanda glanced at her hands folded in her lap, trying not to betray her anger. She didn't want him to know she'd been snooping.

"Mr. Bradshaw is unable to meet with Mrs.

Grenshaw on her time table, so I switched your assignment over to him, and you can take his."

Amanda stood, her face heating. "Randolph, how could you give away my assignment?"

"I told you…" he sputtered.

"Not a good enough explanation." She stepped to his desk, propping her hands on a stack of papers. "You gave him my assignment because he's a man."

"Not true." His face colored. "If he was able to meet with Mrs. Grenshaw—"

"He didn't want to meet with Mrs. Grenshaw!" Amanda pointed a finger at Randolph. "He refused to take the assignment and demanded another."

"How did you know…?" Randolph's dark eyes widened. "You tricked me!"

Amanda straightened her spine and folded her arms across her chest. "Because you lied to me."

"My love…" He stood, reaching for her. "I can't appear to show you favoritism just because we're courting."

Amanda turned her back to him. "I can remedy that."

He stepped to her side. His hands slid around her waist and shoulder as he guided her back to the chair. "You don't mean what I think you do."

"What I mean is, we should stop courting, then you won't be showing me favoritism. I'll be just another employee."

"Amanda, please…" He kneeled on the floor beside the chair and grasped her hands. "I care too deeply for you to allow it to end. And I know you like working here."

"But if you can't treat me fairly, I'd be better off

working elsewhere." She drew her hands from his and turned away.

Randolph sighed and stood. He glanced toward the door, obviously hoping his other employees hadn't caught him groveling. "I don't want you to be angry with me. In fact, I have a surprise for you."

Amanda shrugged. Though intrigued, she didn't want to let on that he'd snagged her attention.

"After we close the office tonight, I'll take you to dinner, and then I'll show you my surprise."

"I don't know." Amanda glanced at her hands. "My father would be upset if we don't have a chaperone." She looked up. "Or would we?"

"Amanda…" He sighed. "I care a great deal about you and would never harm or compromise you." He stepped close and lifted her chin. His dark eyes held hers. "It's a present…for you."

"But must we wait until after dinner to see it?" She frowned.

"I promise you, it will be well worth the wait."

****

Carver, Pennsylvania
Present Day

Jack Lawton brushed aside a food wrapper from last night's meal and stepped from his shabby compact to survey the dilapidated Victorian house.

"Hey, dude," a male voice called. "Be right with you."

Jack stared at the porch where a young man with long, sandy-colored hair and a goatee stood, leaning over the railing. This couldn't possibly be the new owner. He had to be a younger brother or son of the man he'd spoken to on the phone.

Unzipping his hooded sweat jacket, Jack exposed his T-shirt. He'd decided to meet Shane Bradley in casual clothes to provide a workmanlike appearance. Once he got to work on the renovations, he wouldn't exactly be showing up in a suit or even sports jacket. If he got the job.

Six months before, he'd been set to start renovations for Mrs. Grayson, a widow who had lived alone but had a nest egg of money socked away from her late husband's business. She'd lived in the house since she was a girl and wanted to restore it to its former splendor. She'd met with Jack, stuffing him with tea and cakes, gushing over his ideas for her home. She'd then led him on tour of the small, quaint house. He'd marveled at all the antiques she'd acquired, including a silver-framed tintype photograph of a beautiful young woman with soulful eyes. The old woman claimed she was an ancestor who once lived in the house in the late nineteenth century.

Jack stepped up the walk to shake hands with Bradley. "I'm glad you agreed to meet with me here. I'm sorry about your grandmother. She seemed like a great lady."

Bradley shrugged. The oversized white T-shirt he wore billowed out over his slim figure. He didn't look like he was old enough to be out of high school.

The young man scratched his goatee and waved his other arm toward the house. "This place is a dump. I just want to get rid of it." He waggled his light-colored brows. "Now, if you wanted to buy it, I'd give you a good price."

Jack's blood heated at the offer. If only he had the money for a down payment, but his present finances wouldn't permit him to move out of the small studio he paid a fortune to rent, leaving him little money for anything else. This job would've given him the impetus to consider starting a business of his own—on the side, of course, until he built up a decent clientele.

He'd spent hours drawing pictures, helped Mrs. Grayson pick out colors, and now wished the house belonged to him. What he wouldn't give to own a beautiful old home. But his plans had gone to shit when Mrs. Grayson suffered a massive heart attack and died on the spot. Although his boss now had Jack and his crew working on the renovation of a supermarket, his heart wasn't in his current job. But he needed the money.

He sighed. "I wish I could. This is a beautiful, old house, and if you didn't want to live here, you'd still make out renting or even selling it after renovations. You'd fetch top price, I'm sure."

He glanced toward the car in the driveway. A shabby old compact much like what Jack drove. But maybe his grandma had left him a pile of cash along with the house, so he could afford renovations. All Jack could do was hope.

Bradley shook his head. "I want to sell and get out now. My band has a gig on the west coast next month, and I need cash to live on. You know how it is."

The young man caught Jack's gaze. He knew exactly how it was in this economy to make ends meet, but to let this house go for near nothing galled him.

"You know, it'll take time to sell this, even as a handyman special."

"I don't plan to sell it, man." Bradley turned toward the open window. "I'm selling the land. Already have a potential buyer. They plan to demolish this place and build three new homes."

Jack's blood chilled. "It's going to be demolished?"

"Grandma left me enough cash, and I made more selling a lot of her stuff. The place is cleaned out and ready for the demo team. The new owner already has it set up."

"It's already sold?" Jack's heart sank. This trip had obviously been for nothing. The kid had already decided the grand old home's fate.

"Settlement's next week. Once I get my money, I don't give a shit what happens to it. I'll be living on the west coast."

"I see." Jack swallowed. "Would you mind if I had a last look around? I put in a lot of work planning the renovation."

Bradley shrugged. "Sure, dude. Take your time." He waved Jack through the door.

His footsteps echoed on the empty wood floors of the foyer and living room. When he'd been here last, the place had been furnished with a room sized wool rug and antique furniture befitting the surroundings. Lamps on end tables had glowed softly as he and Mrs. Grayson looked over his drawings and ideas for the house.

Now, it was empty. Everything had been stripped, including the glass chandelier from the dining area. He glanced along the empty wall toward the staircase. A silver frame caught his attention. He strode toward the bottom step. The woman's wide eyes seemed fixed on him, her full lips slightly parted.

Jack turned back toward Bradley, who stood

behind him. A frown creased the young man's forehead. "Must have missed this one."

Jack glanced up the staircase. All of the other photographs were gone. The only evidence they'd been here, rectangles of lighter color along the peeling striped wallpaper. He turned back to the photo, transfixed by the image.

"What do you plan to do with it?" Jack asked.

Bradley shrugged. "What I did with all the others. I sold the frames for scrap and threw the pictures away."

"Threw them away?" Jack's blood heated. "Don't you have any family who would want them?"

Bradley shook his head. "My folks died two years ago in a car accident. I live with my uncle—my mother's brother—and he doesn't want all this junk."

"I'm sorry to hear about your parents. You're an only child, I take it."

The young man nodded.

Jack glanced at the photo again. Although likely only his imagination, the young woman's gaze seemed to follow him. Almost as if she begged him to take the photo.

"Would it be all right it I took this?" Jack glanced at Bradley. A slight scowl crossed his face. "You can keep the frame," Jack hastily added.

Bradley's scowl changed into a smile. "Deal, dude."

Jack opened the back of the frame, carefully extracted the old photo, and handed the frame to Bradley. "Are you sure you won't change your mind before settlement? With renovations you'd get a good price for it."

The young man's scowl returned. "My uncle just

wants me out of his house as soon as possible. Seems the land is worth more than the house." He glanced toward the living area. "And he wants the settlement to go through before I go."

Jack sighed, wishing again he could buy the property before settlement took place next week. He was sure he'd never convince the new owners to renovate when they were bent on building new homes.

He tucked the photo into his jacket to protect it, then offered his hand to Bradley. "Sorry to disturb you then. Good luck with your gig on the coast."

Bradley broke into a wide smile. "Thanks, dude. Sorry you came out for nothing." He escorted Jack onto the porch.

"Oh, no," Jack said, patting the photo to be sure it was secure. "I didn't come for nothing."

Chapter Two

Jack stared at the television screen, but his brain didn't connect to the program. His thoughts strayed to the Victorian house. The idea of it being demolished to make way for new homes grated on his nerves. He'd racked his brain earlier this evening, trying to figure a way to borrow enough cash to make a down payment. But even if he did, then what? He simply didn't earn enough to get a mortgage.

The photo he'd taken from the house sat propped on his desk beside his PC monitor. Even in the subdued lamplight, he could make out the woman's features. Her hair of a light, indeterminate color piled on her head, a few delicate tendrils framed her face.

What intrigued him so about this woman? She was long dead, a ghost. His latest girlfriend had left him six months before. She'd lived with him about a year, then decided she had to go to California to find herself. She hadn't asked him to go with her. Not that he would've. Their relationship had fizzled out the last few months. When she talked to him, it had been to complain about his lack of ambition. She didn't understand why he was satisfied with his underling job and why he was content to sit home night after night. She worked as a waitress, but her dream was to be an actress.

Weeks before she broke the news, he'd already moved on in his mind and had the feeling she'd already found another man to replace him. They'd said goodbye, and she was gone from his apartment, his life, and his dreams.

He clicked the remote to turn off the TV, then padded into the bathroom for a quick shower. Afterward, he opened the futon, preparing to jump into bed, but he needed to look at the photo one more time.

"If only I could meet someone like you," he told the picture. "But you're from another world, a simpler time." He raked a hand through his hair. "Now I'm talking to photos. Go to sleep, Jack." He carefully propped the picture back on his desk and settled on the bed, reaching over to set the alarm for the morning.

He drifted to sleep with the image of the woman seated on a bench in a Victorian garden.

"Jack?"

He glanced up into the most incredible blue eyes. Like sapphires.

"Excuse me?"

The woman shook her head, the large blue flowers atop her hat bobbing. "You promised me a tour of our house." Her full lips quirked upward.

He swallowed. This was the woman in the photo, but instead of a black and white tintype, he was gazing at a beautiful, flesh and blood woman. Her reddish-gold hair was piled up under her hat, a few loose tendrils curled past her ears. A high-necked gown draped over her legs, completely covering her toes. Seated in an outdoor gazebo, she watched him intently.

"I've been waiting so long to see it finished." She reached out a gloved hand and motioned for him to sit.

Her eyes so mesmerized him, he brushed against the gazebo pillar, nearly losing his balance. Her bright smile drew a grin from him.

Before he sat, he glanced over his shoulder. This was the house! The one being demolished, but it was new.

"Where am I?" he demanded of the woman. "And who are you?"

"Jack, are you quite all right?" Her smile faded into a frown. "I'm Amanda. I rescued you."

"Huh?"

A loud buzz pulled him away. He jerked upright.

"What the hell?" He rubbed his face. His subconscious had mixed the photo and the house into a crazy dream.

Collapsing onto the bed, he groaned. He glanced toward the window, noting the sky was still dark, the streetlights still on. The last thing he felt like doing was going back to work on a remodel of a supermarket, but he needed the paycheck. Bad.

He pushed himself off the bed and grabbed a shirt to slip over his head. On the way to the bathroom, he clicked on the lamp, and his gaze fell on the photo of the woman. The woman in the dream said her name was Amanda. Maybe after work, he'd do a little investigating to see if he could find out who had lived in the house prior to the twentieth century.

As he washed his face, his pulse raced. He stared into the mirror. Waiting until the workday was done would be practical, but he realized he had to know now. He had to go back to the house, before it was torn down.

He grabbed his phone and punched in his boss's number. "Hey, Ron," he said when the man picked up. "I'm really sick. Don't think I can make it in today."

Ron sighed. "Okay. You feel that bad, I think we can make do."

Jack held back his sigh of relief. He wouldn't be happy with a short paycheck next week, but he had to go to the house today. He couldn't explain it.

"Thanks, Ron."

"If you don't think you can make it tomorrow, call me tonight, so I can find a few temp helpers to add to the work crew."

"Okay, I will. Thanks again." Jack closed his cell and leaned against the wall, still not sure why he'd felt impelled to call out.

He stepped to the counter and rinsed his coffee pot in the sink. After a cup of coffee and whatever he could find in the fridge to eat, he'd drive to the house and have a look around.

After gulping the last mouthful of coffee, he stepped toward his desk and the photo of the young woman. On impulse, he stuffed the picture into his inside jacket pocket.

An hour later, he walked up to the porch of the house on the corner of Wendover Street. He glanced up and down the block. The few people strolling by took no notice of him. He knocked, but was sure Shane Bradley wasn't around this early in the morning. Problem was, he couldn't gain access to the inside if the man wasn't in. After a few minutes, he heaved a sigh and turned to go. He had Bradley's cell number. Maybe he could call him.

But an intuitive hunch made him spin back to the door. He tried the knob, and the door creaked open. He glanced around once again to be sure no one watched him. The last thing he needed was cops showing up to arrest him for trespassing.

The door opened inward, inviting him to enter. Slipping through the threshold, he gently closed the door and leaned against it.

What the hell am I doing?

He crept into the living area, careful not to let his boots echo in the empty house. The nearest neighbor shouldn't be close enough to hear, but he didn't want to take any chances.

As if drawn along on a rope, he approached the stairs and planted his hand on the empty spot where the photo had hung. Vibrations shot up his arm. He snatched his hand away, his heart racing.

A vision of the woman in the photo, the one from his dream, sent his pulse hammering. He imagined pulling the hat from her head, freeing her red-gold hair, and running his fingers through the silken strands, while she sighed with pleasure.

"This is nuts!" He continued up the stairs, careful not to make more than a slight creak as he moved steadily upward. If he were caught in here, he'd end up in jail for sure. And who would bail him out?

At the upstairs landing, he stepped from the window, careful not to expose himself. If anyone outside saw him, they'd likely think he was the owner or a workman, but why take a chance? He'd have a quick look around, then get the hell out of here.

He opened the door to one of the rooms. It was large, completely empty. The master bedroom. He stepped down the hall, opening the next door. Another empty room. A door a foot down opened into a bathroom. That left one more at the end of the hall, the rear of the house.

Before he reached for the knob, the handle turned. The door opened inward. Jack's heart thundered. He jumped back, expecting to be ambushed.

After a long moment of silence, he crept to the doorway.

"Anyone here?" he asked. "I won't give you any trouble. I'm just looking the house over." A vagrant squatter might panic and rush him to get away.

He eased himself through the doorway. "I won't hurt you or force you out. I swear."

Nothing but silence. His breath caught, and the back of his neck prickled in the eerie quiet. He raised his hands but wondered if he shouldn't just get the hell out of here.

Forcing himself to breathe, he crept into the room, fully prepared to ward off any attack. But none came. He checked every corner of the room. No built-in closets to hide in, so who opened the door?

He stepped to the window and gazed out. Too high for someone to have escaped this way. He glanced back at the door, half expecting it to slam shut, trapping him inside.

He rubbed his arms. A sudden chill gripped him. *Must be nerves.*

He circled the empty room, running his hand along the walls. In spots, the wallpaper and plaster had literally rotted away, exposing rotted wood beams. If only he'd had the chance to restore this house. He'd have done Mrs. Grayson proud.

"Enough self-pity," he said aloud. "Time to go."

He stepped to the doorway, but a creak followed by a groaning and a loud crack, stayed him.

Something hard and heavy clipped his head. Pain

radiated like a white-hot light, and he fell.

****

April 6, 1881

By day's end, Amanda begged off Randolph's invitation, claiming a headache. In truth, after he'd given away the coveted assignment, she couldn't abide sitting for hours across the table from the man.

When he grasped her hand, she tried her best not to recoil.

"I'm sorry you're not feeling well, my dear. Perhaps another time. But I do want to tell you about my surprise, if you could sit for just a minute, then I'll see you home."

Amanda gritted her teeth but slid into the seat he indicated at the side of his desk. "Randolph, I really don't think—"

He cut her off. "I'm building a home on Wendover Street. It's nearly complete."

"A—a home?" Amanda didn't understand why he thought this important to her, but then it dawned like a brick wall falling on her head.

"I plan to speak to your father." He lifted her hand and brushed his lips over her knuckles. Amanda's breath quickened, but not with desire. She wanted to snatch her hand back, escape his office this minute.

"I'd like to show it to you tomorrow, if it's all right," he continued. "I'll see you home then call on you before lunch."

"I—I'm not sure how I'll be feeling by morning."

He patted her hand. "I'll put in a few hours at the office then come to see how you're doing."

She nodded, although she had the urge to shout at him. Her father would be at the bank, though, so

Randolph would have no chance to converse with him at least. He obviously wanted to ask Father for her hand.

All she wanted for now was to get home and crawl into bed. She didn't want to speak to anyone, even her own family about her boss's interest toward her. Although she knew her stepmother would be sympathetic to her plight, her father would likely deem this a fortuitous match for his daughter. But she wasn't sure someone as old-fashioned as Randolph was what she wanted for a husband. She longed for a forward-thinking man like her father, who treated women as equals, not property. He'd always allowed her stepmother to speak her mind.

Amanda aspired to be just like her.

Randolph insisted on walking her home, but as they reached the door, she thanked him and said goodbye.

"But," he protested, "I should see you inside at least."

She patted his wool clad arm. "I just want to go right to bed. I think a good night's sleep will help me get rid of my headache."

He frowned. "If you insist. I would never force my way into your home…but—"

She grasped the knob and opened the door, stopping his protests with a smile. "I'll be fine."

Once inside, she gently closed the door in his face and leaned her back against it. Footsteps outside told her he'd left. She stepped to the window and peered through the gauze curtain, staying back, so he wouldn't see her watching.

He descended the porch steps and eased out the

front gate, looking back once. She ducked back, then took a quick peek. He strode down the road.

Amanda let out the breath she'd been holding and stepped to the kitchen. Despite her claim of a headache, what she really wanted was something in her stomach.

She found no one in the large room full of comforting cooking smells. Her father and brother were likely still at the bank, and Mrs. O'Leary hadn't arrived to start dinner. She wasn't sure where her stepmother was, likely out and about at this hour.

Amanda discovered a few biscuits left over from lunch or breakfast in a crock and stuffed them into her mouth. The snack would hold her for now. She really didn't want to speak to either of her parents tonight. She'd take a book to her room and turn in early. Curiosity caused a sudden urge to find Randolph's house in the morning before he had a chance to call on her.

The front door creaked open as she reached the stairs. Her stepmother stood at the threshold holding a sack. She smiled at Amanda as she set the bag down. Pulling out a hat pin, she removed her felt hat revealing her red-gold hair, so like Amanda's own hair color.

"Amanda," she said, "I didn't expect anyone to be home yet. I told Mrs. O'Leary not to start dinner until six, since your father and brother won't be home until seven."

"I'm not feeling well, Mother. I have a bit of a headache." She held up the book she planned to read. "I'll just read for a while, then go to sleep."

Her stepmother strode forward and placed her palm on Amanda's brow.

"Mother," she protested, "I don't have a fever, just

a headache. I'll be perfectly fine after a good night's sleep."

"Go ahead." She waved her arm for Amanda to proceed up the stairs. "I'll check on you after dinner and see if you'd like something to eat."

"Thank you." Amanda nodded.

Once her stepmother turned toward the kitchen, Amanda ascended the stairs. After a few hours of reading, Amanda's eyes refused to stay open. She prepared for bed and climbed under the covers.

Although tired, Amanda tossed, not able keep the image of Randolph's face from her mind. Her door opened, Erin's lavender scent drifting into the room, but Amanda relaxed, keeping her eyes closed and breathing even. The door closed again. She punched her pillow and rolled over, finally drifting into an uneasy sleep.

She woke to sunlight bleeding through the drawn curtains. The clock showed nine. Sighing, she rose and quickly dressed, wishing she'd awakened earlier. She'd not allow Randolph to call on her before she made her escape to see the house on her own.

She stopped at the bottom of the stairs. Voices rose from the kitchen, likely her family finishing breakfast. She strode to the door and pinned her hat on and wrapped a shawl around her shoulders.

Slipping out the door, she hurried down the path, hoping her family wouldn't catch sight of her and inquire as to where she was going. Today was her regular day off from the newspaper office. If they found her missing, they'd likely think she'd gone shopping.

She inhaled the fresh spring air on this sunny, cloudless day. Fragrant tree buds stood out on the oaks lining the streets. Daffodils and tulips decorated gardens and flower boxes. Sparrows chattered in the trees overhead.

Wendover Street lay a few blocks from her home. As she strolled down the sidewalk, she looked for any homes under new construction. Finally at the corner of the street, she found it, a three story home with a wraparound porch. The clapboard siding had yet to be painted, and the grounds, void of landscaping, contained mounds of dirt and patches of missing grass. Big windows with hand-blown glass appeared naked without any curtains or shades. This must be it. She sauntered past, studying the house. No sounds of hammers or saws rose from inside, nor did she hear voices. Maybe the workmen weren't working today or hadn't yet arrived.

She drew close to the porch, straining her ears for any sound. The last thing she wanted to do was run into a disgruntled workman or, worse, Randolph.

Glancing up and down the street to be sure no one saw her, she drew in a breath and turned the door knob. The door opened inward. She stepped inside, inhaling the inviting scent of fresh cut wood. She didn't want to announce her presence for fear of being sent away. Something about this house beckoned to her.

She stepped through the foyer into a short hall with a staircase on the right side. Again, she strained her ears, alert to any sound. Setting one foot on the stairs, she decided them to be sound and climbed. In the hall, she hesitated, wondering why the urge to explore so compelled her. If anyone caught her, she'd just tell them Randolph had invited her to see the house but hadn't yet arrived.

Emboldened by the idea, she stepped down the

hall, poking her head into a large room. None of the rooms had attached doors yet. This, likely, was the master bedroom. She suppressed a shudder, knowing Randolph held intentions of sharing it with her.

Another room in the center of the hall lay unoccupied as well. She stepped toward the back room. Through the doorway, she noted parts of the inner wall yet unfinished, and the floor didn't appear entirely stable. She'd take a quick look then leave before Randolph even knew she'd been here.

As she peered around the corner, she gasped at the sight of a man sprawled across the floor. Dressed in shirtsleeves and work britches, sleeves rolled up to his elbows, he must be a workman.

"Hello," she called, unsure of what to do. She shouldn't be here, after all, but she couldn't just leave the poor man. What if he were dead?

Her hand rose to her throat at the thought. She took a deep breath and strode forward, but a creak in the floor stopped her. If the floor wasn't finished, she risked the chance of falling through to the floor below.

She tested the floor inside the room with one foot and then the other. The man lay sprawled on his stomach, a large beam beside him. She lifted her skirts to step over the beam and knelt at the man's side, feeling his neck for a pulse.

A steady beat throbbed under her fingers. She breathed a sigh of relief.

Now, what do I do?

Blood matted the man's short, sandy-colored hair. *Likely a blow from the beam.* She touched the spot gently, noting a raised knot. His face lay turned to the side. She glanced around the room for something she could use to stanch the flow of blood. Her gaze alighted on a rag near him. After grabbing it, she pressed it against his head. If she turned him onto his side, she could check for other injuries and help him breathe more easily.

Using all her strength, she pushed him over and tilted her ear toward his mouth. Shallow breaths lifted his broad chest that rose and fell with regularity. If only she could wake him.

Sandy lashes brushed against his cheek. The urge to run her hand over his firm, clean-shaven jaw caused her cheeks to heat.

She'd have to leave him and find help.

As she rose to go, an ever-so-slight sound drew her attention. His eyes fluttered open.

Chapter Three

Jack blinked. Blinding pain in the back of his head nearly caused him to pass out again. The last thing he recalled was a beam blindsiding him.

"Sir?" a female voice cooed. "What's happened? Did the beam hit you?"

He tried to focus on a face hovering above him. "Yeah, the beam hit me. It must have knocked me out." He lifted his arm, intending to probe his aching head.

"Don't move," the woman said. "I have a rag covering the gash. You need a doctor, I think."

He gazed at the woman. With her red-gold hair piled on her head and her old-fashioned looking gown, she didn't seem real. Like something out of a crazy dream. If her face wasn't so smooth and youthful, he'd believe he was back at Mrs. Grayson's house, but the old woman was dead, and she'd never dressed like this.

"Where am I?" he groaned. A flash of pain shot through his skull.

The woman's blue eyes widened. "You don't know where you are? The beam must have taken your memory." She glanced around. "This house is under construction. You're obviously one of the workmen hired to build it."

"Under construction?" A new wave of pain pierced his skull. "No. This house is going to be torn down."

"Shh." She placed a finger over his lips. "You must

have had a memory lapse."

Her soft touch and scent enveloped him. Something seemed familiar about her, but he wasn't sure what. He tried to rise, but she pushed him back.

"Don't try to get up. I'll go for help."

"No." He rubbed his head. "I think I can sit up with your assistance." Pushing onto his elbows, he gazed around the room. His heart dropped as he realized this wasn't the dilapidated house he'd been exploring. The scent of fresh cut wood and unfinished walls chilled him.

"You say this house is under construction?" He made an effort to sit up straight.

She moved to brace his back. "You mustn't move so quickly. You could aggravate your injury."

"This doesn't make any sense." He reached for the towel she'd placed against the back of his head. The rag slid down his back.

She retrieved it, then gently probed his head.

He winced at the pain.

Her gaze met his. "It doesn't look so bad now. The bleeding's stopped, but you will need someone to look after you. I'll contact your family."

"There's no need. I can drive. Just help me to my car. It's parked outside."

"Car?" She bit her lip, drawing his attention to her full, ripe mouth. "You mean carriage? I saw no carriage outside."

"No, I mean a car. It's a dark green four-door."

"I saw no carriage as you describe." She wrung her hands glancing toward the open doorway. "I'll go find help."

His hand shot out to stop her. He didn't want her to

go, even to get help. If he was able to stand...

"Help me up," he said.

She frowned but grasped his hand. Pushing up on his legs with her assistance at his side, he stood. But his equilibrium seemed off. She braced her weight against his.

"Are you sure you don't want to stay here? I'll find a neighbor to help you to go..." She hesitated. "Where do you want to go?"

"Home, but I need my car to get there." His hand dropped to his pocket to search for his wallet, but a strap and two buttons on his waistband diverted his attention. He wore a pair of suspenders, a loose fitting shirt with four buttons reaching from his mid-chest area to his collar, and baggy wool pants. These weren't the clothes he'd been wearing when he'd explored the house.

What the hell?

His alarmed gaze drifted down to the woman who still supported his weight. The clothes he wore matched the period of her gown. And the condition of the house, compared to the dilapidated building he'd been in, set his brain awhirl.

"Where in hell am I?" he gasped.

The woman's eyes widened as she gazed openmouthed at him. "Please let me get you help, sir."

"Not until I see my car," he growled. "Get me down the stairs."

Between his spinning head and the knowledge that something was very wrong, he had difficulty descending the steps. For one thing, the stairway had no railing. He pressed a hand against the wall, the woman on his other side, but he feared knocking her over the edge.

He inched his way down and breathed a sigh of relief when they reached bottom.

"Please, sir, sit here on the bottom step for at least a moment to catch your breath. I'd hate to see you start bleeding again or pass out."

He did as she bid, cradling his face in his hands. His head still spun, and he wasn't sure he could make it home after all. Maybe he should have her call an ambulance.

Her footsteps sounded hollow on the unfinished wood floor as she paced. He lifted his gaze to study her. Her skirts nearly touched the freshly sanded floor as she braced her hands on either side of her hips. Her brow furrowed, lips twisted into an expression of anxiety.

"I'm sorry," he said.

She turned and faced him. "Sorry?"

"For putting you to all this trouble." He realized he didn't even know his rescuer's name. "I'm Jack Lawton, by the way, and you are…?"

She pursed her full lips. "Miss Montgomery."

"You don't have a first name?" he asked.

"Sir, we are strangers to one another." Her face reddened.

"But I gave you my first name." He spread his hands.

She propped her hands on her hips. "My father would have a conniption fit if I gave my Christian name to a strange man. On the other hand, my stepmother…" Her lips curved into the hint of a smile. "…always introduces herself by her first name to the consternation of my father." She lifted her chin as if appraising Jack. "I'm Amanda."

28

Jack smiled but winced as a shot of pain sliced through his skull. "Amanda Montgomery. I'll be sure to remember that name." He lifted his hand. "Now, if you could assist me to the front door."

She stretched her arm down toward him, and he used the wall to hoist himself so he wouldn't put all his weight on her.

A brief wave of dizziness halted his progress, but he steadied himself. "Lead on."

By the time they reached the door, he realized how eerily familiar this house looked. Almost as if the house he'd been in had traveled back in time. Could the new owner have changed his mind and decided to rebuild the place?

Amanda threw open the door.

Jack's mouth gaped. Not only was his car gone, but the entire block was transformed. What had been a paved walk and blacktop street was now packed dirt.

Heat rose to his cheeks. "Where's my car? Did they tow it away to tear up the street?" He couldn't have been unconscious long enough.

"I don't know what you mean." Amanda's gaze scanned the road.

Jack froze in the doorway, not sure what to do. This was insane. He had no car, no cell phone, or ID. If he made it to his house, would it even be there? For one chilling moment, he wasn't sure.

Amanda glanced at him, then back at the road, not saying anything for a long moment. "Mr. Lawton, if you're able to walk a short distance, I'll take you to my home. My stepmother may know how to help you."

"Stepmother?" Jack chewed his lower lip. "And it's Jack, not Mr. Lawton."

Amanda grinned and grasped his arm. Her warmth and scent comforted him. "I'll not call you Jack in front of my parents. At least not my father." She lifted her chin. "And you must call me Miss Montgomery around him."

"Okay." He stepped across the porch following Amanda's lead. For now, he'd stick close to her until he found out what the hell was going on.

****

Amanda supported the workman, Jack, as they made their way to her home. She gulped as a carriage drove down the road, fearing Randolph's presence. The last thing she needed was to have him spy her leading a strange man to her home.

But she couldn't just leave him here. He was hurt and seemed disoriented. And his mention of a car brought back memories of her stepmother's stories. *Stories of the future*. She'd take him to Erin and see if she could make sense of this.

He seemed a bit wobbly, but fortunately, not many people were out and about this time of day. The few who were, openly stared, but at Amanda's nod, they inclined their heads and continued on their way.

She blew out a sigh of relief when they reached her front stoop. Jack lifted his gaze, then grimaced. Apparently his head still pained him, but he made no sound of protest as she led him through the door.

Her father and brother would be at the bank at this hour, but her stepmother might be in. As they entered the foyer, silence yawned from the hall. If home, she'd likely find Erin in the kitchen.

She led Jack to one of the chairs by the staircase. "Sit here a minute. I'll open the parlor doors so you can lie on the settee, then I'll find my stepmother."

He sat with a thump, his tanned, work-roughened hand reaching for his head.

"Does it still hurt?"

He nodded. "A little. You have any ibuprofen by any chance?"

She frowned. "Ibu…I'm not sure what you mean."

He heaved a heavy sigh and sank his face into both hands.

"Just a minute. I'll get you into the parlor."

She flung open the doors and found the parlor empty, as she'd expected. The room was hardly used, except for those rare occasions when a family member entertained guests. But Mrs. O'Leary had cleaned the small room yesterday, so there shouldn't be any dust. She ran her hand over the settee by the fireplace to be sure.

Turning back to the hall, she strode over to Jack. He peered up at her, his eyes bleary. She lifted her hand, and he settled his over hers. His firm, strong grip sent a tingle through her fingers. What would it feel like to have those hands roving over her body? Her face heated at the thought.

She led him to the settee and settled him supine, although his long legs dangled onto the floor. His gaze drifted over the room.

"A lot of stuff in here," he said.

"It's a parlor," she explained.

He frowned, but said nothing more.

"Now you stay put." She propped a pillow behind his head. "I'll see if my stepmother's home."

After a final glance to be sure Jack didn't try to get up, Amanda slipped down the hall and pushed open the kitchen door. Erin sat at the table, furiously scribbling on a pad of paper. A strand of red-gold hair had slipped out of her bun, and the tip of her tongue touched her upper lip. She glanced up at Amanda, her blue eyes wide.

"Amanda, I thought I heard someone come in." She glanced toward the clock set on the pantry. "Too early for your father, anyway." She sighed. "I guess I was really in the zone."

Amanda frowned and shook her head. Since her earliest memories, her stepmother had always uttered strange expressions. Neighbors thought Erin eccentric, but she got along with them all.

"Mother, I need your help," Amanda said.

Erin's brow lifted. "What's wrong?" She set her pad aside and rose.

"I found an injured man." Amanda licked her lips. "He's in our parlor."

"Our parlor?" Erin stepped to the door. "Where did you find him?"

Amanda followed Erin before she could reach the parlor. "I'll explain it all later, but he needs help now. He has a head injury."

Erin glanced back, a frown furrowing her brow. "I'll take a look."

Amanda followed Erin into the parlor, noting Jack still half-reclined, but he looked like he'd tried to sit up. His eyes widened at the sight of her stepmother as she strode to his side.

"Sir," she said. "My daughter told me you have a head injury."

"Yeah," he answered. "Seems a beam connected with my head."

Erin glanced back at Amanda, then at Jack. "You're a workman?"

He nodded but winced. "I work for a contractor."

Erin's lips pursed. "No one was with you when this happened?"

"Ah, no." He grimaced. "The house I was inspecting had just been sold, but it was in a very dilapidated condition. It was scheduled to be demolished. So, I wasn't actually working. I was there on my own."

"I see." Erin turned back to Amanda. "Could you get me a basin and a rag...oh, and some rubbing alcohol? I'd like to take a look at his injury, and it seems he needs a bit of cleaning up."

"Of course, Mother." She wondered if Erin was dismissing her so she could talk to Jack in private, but the blood crusting the back of his head did need attending. She retreated to the kitchen to gather the supplies.

She returned quickly and pushed the door open.

Erin sat on the edge of the settee beside Jack. "You woke up in the unfinished house?" Erin was saying.

"Yeah. Then I saw your daughter hovering over me."

Amanda drew a breath, not sure whether to enter or try to hear more. Before she made up her mind, both their gazes locked on hers, and they withdrew into silence. She had no choice but to enter the room.

She approached them and set the basin with clean water on the table, then handed the rag and alcohol to her stepmother. Erin and Jack exchanged a quick glance, then both focused on Amanda.

"Thanks," Erin said. "If you could turn on your

side, Jack?"

Amanda noted her stepmother's use of his Christian name instead of calling him Mr. Lawton.

"This is going to hurt a bit," Erin said. "I'm sorry."

"No problem," Jack replied.

Amanda bit her lip at the language exchange. Jack seemed to speak in the same unique pattern her stepmother occasionally did.

Erin dipped and wrung out the rag to clean some of the matted blood from Jack's hair, then poured alcohol on the cloth. "You ready?"

"Ready as I'll ever be." His gaze rose to Amanda, and he winked.

Heat rose to her face, and her belly tingled with delight. Although he was a virtual stranger, she felt an instant attraction as well as trust for this man. Of course, her father would never approve of her allowing a common working man to court her.

"Amanda..." Erin glanced toward Jack. "Mr. Lawton will be staying with us for a little while." Her gaze lifted. "Could you prepare Billy's bed for him? We'll find another place for Billy to sleep temporarily."

Amanda's mouth gaped. Her stepmother was giving this stranger her brother's room? She bit her tongue and nodded. "Yes, Mother. I'll do it now."

"Hold on." Jack raised his hand. "I don't want to put anybody out." He frowned at Erin.

Her stepmother reached out and grasped Jack's hand. "You must stay." Her gaze rose to Amanda, and she shrugged. "At least until he recovers. We'd have it no other way."

Amanda glanced from Erin to Jack, then gathered her skirts and headed for the stairs. She had the distinct feeling her stepmother knew more than she was telling about Jack.

Chapter Four

Jack crept up the stairs in the darkened house. At the top lay a hall with a maze of closed doors. He tried each one, but none opened. He grasped the knob of the last door and turned. The door creaked inward to reveal two women in Victorian dress. As he stepped toward them, their flesh melted off to reveal a pair of skeletons.

He leaped back and nearly rolled off the mattress.

His head hurt like hell as he tried to get his bearings in an unfamiliar, half-darkened room. He'd obviously been dreaming, but where was he now?

The memory returned in a flash. He drew up an image of Amanda and her stepmother caring for him in their parlor. Afterward, he must have passed out. He did have a vague memory of being carried somewhere. The women couldn't have brought him to this room, but they did mention Erin's husband and Amanda's brother.

A knock at the door startled him. He half sat up and stared at the closed door.

"Yes," he rasped.

"Mr. Montgomery," a male voice with a Southern drawl replied. "I'd like to speak to you, if I may?"

Jack swallowed. "Come in," he managed.

A tall man with dark brown hair entered the room. He wore a waistcoat and suspenders, and carried a lantern.

Despite his aching head, Jack propped himself up against the headboard.

"Forgive me for disturbing you." The man set the lantern on the table beside Jack's bed. "I'm Amanda's father. I spoke to my wife and daughter, and they told me your story. You'd passed out by the time I arrived home, so my son and I carried you up here." He gazed intently at Jack. "You look rather pale, son."

"My head's throbbing." Jack pressed his fingers against his temples. "This is your son's room? How long have I been here?" He glanced around noting the furnishings in the lantern light. He sat on a narrow bed, with a small table, a dresser, and a small wardrobe against the wall opposite.

"I'm afraid you've been in and out of it for days, son. I'll have my wife bring up a cold compress and some headache power. I think you could do with some soup as well."

"Days?" Jack blinked a few times, trying to dispel the pain enough to see and converse. He needed to know just what the hell was going on.

"I'll leave the lantern." The man turned toward the door.

"No, wait," Jack said.

Montgomery turned back, frowning.

"If you could give me some answers. I don't know where I am or how I got here."

Montgomery raised his hand. "My wife will be more of a help to you in that regard than I. She came to me from a different place, too."

"What do you mean?" Jack's pulse raced. "How did she get here?" He struggled to sit up straighter and drop his feet to the floor, but his limbs felt like a wrung out mop.

"Please, sir, wait for my wife. She can explain this better than I. I'll send her up right away." The man stepped to the door and eased himself through, closing it behind him.

Jack slipped to the edge of the bed to try to follow, but a wave of dizziness caused him to flop back onto the mattress.

How the hell am I going to find my way back home?

****

Amanda stepped into the kitchen. Her stepmother sat at the table conversing with the cook. Mrs. O'Leary was a stout, gray-haired Irish woman who her father had employed as a cook and housekeeper after the family had moved from Philadelphia. Amanda had only been ten years old when they'd come to Carver, but her earliest memories centered around her grandparents' house in North Carolina before her father married Erin just after the war. She was only six at the time. Five years after the move to Philadelphia, they'd relocated to this small Pennsylvania town. Mrs. O'Leary was hired to help her mother out with the cooking and housework as well as the care of her baby brother, Billy.

"Miss Amanda." Mrs. O'Leary turned from the sink and propped a plump hand on her hip. "Tell me how it is you found the poor young man your ma's told me about."

"I…ah…" Amanda met her stepmother's warning gaze. "I was walking by the new house they're building on Wendover Street. I heard a terrible crash and went in to investigate."

Erin bit her lip, but nodded.

Amanda continued. "I found him lying on the floor unconscious, his head bleeding. I was able to revive him and wanted to get help, but he insisted I take him home." She spread her hands. "But he couldn't remember where he lived."

"Aye." The cook nodded solemnly as she stirred eggs in a bowl. "A head injury could very well cause a man to forget many things."

"I told Mrs. O'Leary we thought to keep him here at least for a few days," Erin said, "until he recovers from his injuries and regains his wits."

"A wise decision, ma'am." The older woman clicked her tongue. "I wonder if he's one of the Macmillan boys. They work construction around this part of town."

Erin shook her head. "I don't believe so." She shot Amanda a warning glance.

The door creaked open. Billy stepped into the kitchen snatching one of the blueberry muffins Mrs. O'Leary had cooling on the sideboard.

The cook swatted at him. "Mind your manners, young man."

"Billy…" Erin shook her head, but a small smile played about her lips.

Amanda had seen that look before. Billy was Erin's only natural child and over the years, she coddled the boy, much to her father's consternation.

Billy resembled their father with his dark hair and tall, lean build. Amanda suspected that was another reason her stepmother was so soft on her brother. Too soft for his own good, her father was fond of saying.

"I've bacon and eggs for your breakfast, lad." Mrs. O'Leary motioned to the pan on the stovetop.

"Don't have time," Billy insisted. "Have to get to the bank early." He popped the muffin in his mouth and slipped out the door.

Amanda gathered her skirts and sat across the table from her stepmother. "He said his name is Jack Lawton."

Mrs. O'Leary shook her head. "Don't recall anyone by that name." She stepped to the table and served bacon and eggs on each plate. "Won't the Mister be joining you for breakfast, ma'am?"

Erin waved her hand. "If he graces us with his presence, he can serve himself. You go on and eat."

The woman smiled. "Don't mind if I do."

Amanda grew up with her stepmother's cavalier attitude regarding the help. Although her father paid Mrs. O'Leary's salary, Erin insisted the woman sit down to meals with them. She also refused to eat in the formal dining room set off from the kitchen, unless they were entertaining guests.

As a result, Amanda had always thought of the cook as a sort of older relation, calling her Auntie Ida when she was small.

After a cordial breakfast, Mrs. O'Leary cleared the table and plopped a kettle on the stove to heat water for washing dishes. Amanda saw this as her opportunity.

"Mother, before I leave for work, I'd like to have a word with you in the parlor."

Erin quirked a brow but nodded. With the cook occupied at the sink, she gathered her skirts and followed Amanda from the room.

At the parlor door, Erin frowned. "Is there a problem, Amanda?"

She nodded and opened the door to the empty

room. She had to find out the truth about Jack and was sure Erin knew more than she admitted.

Motioning her stepmother to take a seat on the settee, Amanda waited, tapping her foot.

Erin sighed, eyeing her. "So, tell me what's wrong."

"Where did Jack come from, Mother?" Amanda propped both hands on her hips.

Erin spread her hands. "How would I know? From his clothing and the place you found him, he must be a workman. But I don't understand why no one else was in the house at the time. He surely wouldn't have been working alone." She shook her head. "And he doesn't seem to remember anything except his name."

Amanda bit her lip. "I don't believe you, Mother. I heard you and Jack talking upstairs."

Erin's eyes widened, but she said nothing.

"He was saying something about the future. And he also uses those phrases peculiar only to you."

"Amanda, I told you those were only stories I made up to entertain you when you were a child."

"So I believed. But no longer. You have a connection with Jack."

"I never met the man before. I swear." Erin raised her hand.

The door creaked open, startling Amanda. Her father stood in the foyer.

"Something wrong, Will?" Erin asked.

Her father stepped into the room. "I was just upstairs with Jack. He needs attending to."

"I'll go." Erin stood. "There are breakfast leavings in the kitchen if you're hungry."

He nodded. "I'll get a quick bite, then I have to get

to the bank." He stepped forward and kissed Erin on the lips.

Her stepmother's face flushed. "See you tonight."

Her father pecked Amanda's cheek, then stepped out, leaving the door ajar.

Amanda grasped Erin's arm. "I'll see to Jack, Mother."

Erin's brows rose. "Nonsense. You get yourself ready for work. I'll take care of Jack."

Amanda scowled. "But they can do without me for a half hour. You can get started on your new book."

Erin opened her mouth but hesitated. "I'll have plenty of time to work after I take care of him."

Amanda huffed and left the room. She'd catch her father before he left for the bank but intended to see Jack and question him further.

She found her father in the kitchen, sampling a slice of bacon. "I'll be more than glad to heat up the leftover eggs for you, sir," Mrs. O'Leary said.

"I'm fine, Mrs. O'Leary." When her father turned in Amanda's direction, his dark brows rose. "I thought you'd be readying to leave for the paper."

"I wanted to speak to you first."

Both the cook and her father frowned.

"I'll finish up in here, sir, then be about my chores," the cook said.

"I take it Billy's already left."

"That he has. He's a bright and eager lad." She wiped her hands on her apron. "I'd wager he'll be earning more than you before long."

Her father winked. "Could be."

"Father…" Amanda grasped his wool clad arm. "If we could speak now."

"Yes." He turned to face her.

"Not here. Outside."

He shrugged. "If you wish."

Mrs. O'Leary continued cleaning up the kitchen, but Amanda was sure the woman had sharp hearing.

"Good day, Mrs. O'Leary," her father said in way of departure.

"Good day to you, sir."

Amanda led her father to the door. The parlor doors were closed, and she didn't see Erin, so assumed she'd gone upstairs to see to Jack.

Her father stepped through the entry door and she followed, closing the door behind her. Amanda inhaled the fresh spring air as sunshine bathed her upturned face, promising a lovely day.

"Is something wrong, Amanda? Are you having problems at the paper…or with Randolph?"

"No, Father…I want to speak to you about Jack."

Her father shrugged. "I know as much, or maybe less, about him than you."

Amanda frowned. "I'm sorry, Father, but I believe Mother knows more than she's saying. What has she said to you?"

"She thinks his head injury is inhibiting his memory of where he lives and what he was doing before he was hurt. But she said he might remember in time. It's the reason she wanted to take him in for now."

"I think there's more to his story and Mother knows."

"Amanda, I have to get to the bank. If your Mother knows anything more, perhaps you should speak to her."

Amanda crossed her arms over her chest. "If she did know something, she wouldn't tell me. She'd tell you." She pinned her father with a glare.

"Nonsense. You're imagining things, stories your mother told you as a child."

Amanda sighed, knowing she'd get nothing from her father. She turned to step back into the house. At the door, she hesitated and glanced back to find her father frowning. "I'll see you tonight, Amanda."

She nodded, then entered the foyer. Glancing at the staircase, she decided she should try to catch Jack and her stepmother in conversation.

She lifted her skirts and ascended the stairs, being sure to keep her footsteps light. At the top of the staircase, she gazed down the hall. Light filtered into the hallway from Jack's room. Erin stood in the open door holding a tray. Amanda ducked back until she was sure her stepmother had entered the room. Creeping toward the door, Amanda stopped at the edge of the half-open doorway. If Erin caught her, she could just say she was going to her own room.

Voices drifted to her. Erin and Jack.

Chapter Five

Jack opened his eyes. Mrs. Montgomery hovered in the open doorway.

"Jack?" She stepped into the room, carrying a tray. "How are you feeling?"

He slid up on his elbows and fought off a slight wave of dizziness. He'd been lying on his back for days, according to Amanda's father, but no one in this house would let him up, even to relieve himself.

"Ah…" His hand slid to his head. A dull ache still bothered him, but otherwise, he felt a lot better than he had when they'd brought him here. "I think I'm feeling okay. I'd like to try to get up and walk around for a bit."

She nodded. "Good idea." She propped her hands on her hips. "We'll try getting you over to the chamber pot."

"Chamber pot?"

"To relieve yourself," she explained. A grin lighted her face. "It's not like having a bathroom, but it'll have to do. I don't think you'd make it out to the privy in the backyard."

Jack ran a hand over his face. "I'd like to wash up too. How long has it been?"

"Just a few days." She grasped the sheet covering him. "Are you decent under there?"

He glanced beneath the covers at the long

nightshirt Erin had insisted he wear. "I don't usually dress this formally for bed."

She laughed. "Sorry. But with my stepdaughter and Mrs. O'Leary seeing to your needs, it was necessary. Once you're up and about, you can wear whatever you want in the privacy of this room."

"Well, truth be told, the clothes I was wearing when Amanda brought me here weren't mine. Not sure how that happened."

Erin bit her lip. "Let's see if we can get you over to the chamber pot, then we'll talk. I know you have a lot of questions I might have answers to."

Jack nodded and pushed to a seated position in the bed.

Erin yanked up the sheet, and he slid his legs to the floor.

"Now, take it slow," she advised. "I can't have you collapsing on the floor."

He nodded. She stretched out her hands. He grasped hers and with her support, lifted himself to a standing position. His head swam, but after a moment, everything steadied.

"I think I can do this," he said.

She held his arm and step by step led him to a screen in the corner. Glancing around the edge, he caught sight of a large ceramic pot with a lid.

"You want me to go in there?" He turned to meet Erin's gaze.

She laughed again. "I'm sorry. Seems I've gotten used to the way of things over the years. But when I first got here, I was as lost as you."

She pulled a wooden chair over to him. "Hold on to this. I'll give you privacy. Just holler if you need help."

46

His face heated, but he nodded. Once she was out of sight, he took care of business, then replaced the lid on the pot. When he stooped, dizziness threatened to send him sinking onto the chair, but he grasped the back and held on, until it passed.

"I'm finished," he called.

Erin reappeared and glanced at the pot. "You didn't have to replace the lid."

His cheeks burned with embarrassment. "I'm fine."

She nodded. "I'll help you back to the bed. Maybe later, you can try walking a bit further."

He allowed her to lead him to the bed. He sat on the edge, not yet ready to lie down. He'd spent too much time flat on his back and wanted to sit up and talk to this woman.

"You mentioned something about when you first got here." He tilted his head and held her gaze.

She fiddled with her skirts. "Well...I didn't always live here...in this century, I mean."

Jack's pulse raced. "So, you know where I'm from?"

"Not exactly."

"What century is this?"

"The nineteenth. The year is 1881."

"Shit!" Jack folded his arms across his knees. "Sorry."

"No need, Jack. I was as confused and startled when I first woke up here." She leaned forward. "Tell me, do you remember what you were doing right before you woke up in the house?"

"I was in the same house, but in my time. The house was old, dilapidated. It was scheduled to be demolished by the new owner."

"Why were you there?"

He shook his head. "I wasn't supposed to be there at all, but something about the house called to me. I couldn't stand the thought of it being torn down. I wanted to restore it but didn't have the cash to do it. I'd never have qualified for a loan, either." His gaze sought hers. "Amanda's photo was in the house."

Her red-gold brows rose. "Amanda?"

"I'm sure it was her." He glanced away. "If not, a woman who looked just like her."

Erin frowned.

"Whose house is it anyway? It's still under construction."

"Randolph Norwood, Amanda's supervising editor at the newspaper where she works." She pursed her lips. "He wants to court her. I think he has marriage in mind."

Jack's heart sank. "Is he rich?"

Erin smirked. "He's well off, but..." She sighed.

"What? Is he a major butthead or something?"

"He's not exactly the type of man I'd want for my stepdaughter."

"Why not?" Jack sat up straighter.

"He's too old-fashioned. I'm surprised he even hired her as a reporter. She's the only woman working at the newspaper except for his secretary."

"So, I take it you don't like this guy, much."

She grimaced. "I raised Amanda to be her own person. I don't want her to end up married to a man who treats her like property. Men of this period can be so backward in their opinion of women."

A sudden wave of fatigue caused Jack's head to droop.

Erin leaned forward. "Are you feeling all right? Maybe you should lie down for a bit."

Jack shifted on the bed, leaning back on his elbows. Erin rose to lift his legs and adjust his pillows.

"Thanks. I just felt really wiped all of a sudden."

Erin nodded. "You mustn't take it too fast. I'll bring you something to eat, then after you've taken in some food, we'll try getting you up again. For now, I think you should rest."

"No, wait." Jack's hand shot out to stop her. He needed answers to more questions. "I still don't understand why I woke up in those old-fashioned clothes."

She bit her lip. "I'm afraid the same thing happened to me."

He swallowed. "What happened to bring you here?"

"I crashed my car and blacked out." She glanced toward the door. "When I woke up, I was in a tent in a Confederate army camp wearing a gown with blood stains on the collar of the dress. They told me I'd fallen off a horse."

"A horse?"

She nodded. "Seems they knew me as the camp washerwoman, Erin O'Connell."

"How do you explain that?" Jack's head started to throb.

"She was an ancestor of mine. I took over her body."

Heat rose to Jack's face. "What the hell? Are you saying you're in a dead woman's body?"

She lifted her arms in an expansive gesture. "It's all relative. I've come to believe I was Erin O'Connell in a past life. I've just come here to reclaim my body and live my life in a better manner."

Jack frowned. "Past lives? How badly did this ancestor's life go?"

Erin sighed. "Seems she was a Union spy who betrayed Captain Will Montgomery during the war, leading to his death."

"Amanda's father?" Jack's eyes widened.

"And my husband. I've been given a chance to rectify history."

"But if you're in your past-life body, what happened to your body in the future?"

"Originally, I was lying in a hospital in a coma. When I returned, I believe either my future body died or was absorbed into this body."

"Whoa!" Jack raised a hand to his head. "This is getting too weird. Like sci-fi stuff. How do you know you were in a coma? And you said, 'first time'? How many times did you go back and forth?"

"When I first came here, I thought I'd just wake up one day and be in my own time, like waking from a dream. But it took being shot—"

"You were shot?"

"I was trying to prevent Will from being shot, but I took the bullet instead."

Jack drew in a breath. "What happened afterward?"

She spread her hands. "I woke in a hospital bed with tubes attached all over my body. I learned I'd been in a coma since the crash."

A sound at the door drew Jack's attention. Erin glanced at him, her eyes wide, then strode to the doorway.

Chapter Six

Amanda pressed her back against the wall to prevent being seen. So, all those stories her stepmother told Amanda as a child were true!

She'd come from the future and believed Jack did too. Amanda's pulse raced at the implications. How she'd love to see a future time like Erin had described. If there was a way to get there, maybe Jack could take her.

In her excited state, she accidentally thumped her foot against the door frame and drew back with a gasp. Conversation quieted in the room and footsteps approached. She couldn't allow Erin to find her eavesdropping.

She shuffled down the hall and retreated into her own room, swiftly closing the door, although she left it open a crack.

Erin emerged from Billy's room, glancing up and down the hall. Her gaze fixed on Amanda's door. She held her breath, but her stepmother retreated and closed Billy's door.

Amanda breathed a sigh of relief and shut her door completely, being sure not to make any sound. She sat on her bed, trying to absorb what she'd just heard, then clasped her hands together in glee. The future! A place where women were equal to men. A place with horseless carriages, flying machines, and indoor plumbing in every home.

Her father had promised they'd have an indoor bath as soon as it was available in their town, but in the future everyone had this convenience and more. How could Erin stand to live here, when she came from such a fantastic place?

She had to know how Erin was able to move back and forth through time and how Jack got here. If Erin found a way to send him back, Amanda would be first in line to go with him.

All her life she'd felt out of place and longed to be more modern. Maybe Jack was her way to a life she'd never dreamed possible.

****

After Erin departed, Jack sank into the mattress, too weak to do anything but mull over what the woman had told him. If she'd been able to go back and forth through time, he should be able to return. But what if the conk on the head had sent him into a coma? The idea of returning to a comatose body didn't appeal at all. And then, there was Amanda.

Although he'd only just met her, something about her set his pulse racing and his heart fluttering. He must be nuts!

Thankfully, the headache that had plagued him from the time Amanda discovered him lying on the floor had dissipated. The beef soup and homemade bread with butter and raspberry jam Erin brought him for lunch helped as well, but she insisted he only walk as far as the chamber pot. Lying in bed irritated him. If only he had a TV or video game to keep him entertained. He had to get up and out of here as soon as possible.

He tossed in bed, the nightshirt wrapped around his body. How did any man sleep in a thing like this?

Swearing, he lifted the sheet and grasped the hem, yanking the garment up around his waist. He undid the buttons and lifted it over his head, tossing the shirt to the floor.

He breathed a sigh of relief but was now completely naked. With women coming in and out of his room, he'd have to find the clothing he'd arrived in.

Grasping the sheet, he rose slowly. Slight dizziness swept over him, but once he sat upright, it faded. He held the bedpost and stood, wrapping the sheet around his waist. He shuffled across the floor to a chest of drawers. He hoped his clothes hadn't been taken to the wash. Then he'd really be in deep shit.

He opened one of the drawers and found male clothing, although he wasn't sure it was his. Maybe Amanda's brother. Glancing toward the screen, he noticed a pile of folded clothes on top of the dresser.

He stepped toward the clothing but stopped at the sound of a click. His gaze slipped to the door. Someone was turning the knob. He held his breath and clutched the sheet around his waist.

The door cracked, followed by a gasp.

"Sorry. I'm not quite decent," Jack called out.

Amanda stood wide-eyed, staring at him. Instead of apologizing and leaving, she stood gazing in through the partially open door.

Jack grimaced. "I'm trying to find some clothes."

"Where's your nightshirt?" She glanced toward the heap of cloth on the floor by the bed. "Oh!"

"I needed to take it off," Jack explained. "Too confining."

She bit her lip, her eyes bright. Her hand rose to her lips. Was she stifling a giggle?

"Jack…the clothes you were wearing when I found you are on top of the dresser." She bit her lip, peering at him, her gaze lingering on his chest.

He wrapped the sheet tightly around him and stepped toward the dresser. Sorting through the clothes with one hand, holding the sheet with the other, he produced what looked like underpants, although they appeared to be knee-length.

He padded back to the bed, noting Amanda glanced toward the hall. Serve her right if her father caught her spying.

"Are you going to stand there and watch? Why'd you come anyway?"

Amanda swallowed. "Of course not. I just thought I should check on you…to see if you needed anything." She appeared to be suppressing laughter at his predicament.

He shuffled to the bed but turned back once to scowl. "So glad I amuse you," he muttered. "As you can see, I'm fine. You can leave now."

She giggled, then quieted. "I'm sorry, but you do look funny walking about in a sheet."

"You wouldn't think it was so funny if I dropped it." He plopped onto the bed.

Her face turned beet red. "You wouldn't dare," she challenged.

He grinned. "Don't bet on it." Grasping the garment, he examined it. Except for the lack of an elastic band at the top, he'd take these for underwear, although a bit long. Two buttons provided closure at the waist.

"Those are the clothes you wore when I brought you here."

He frowned. "Who took them off me…and why?"

She blushed. "Well, they needed to be washed…and so did you."

"You mean…" The thought of her undressing and washing him wasn't too embarrassing, unless it wasn't her, but…

"I didn't do it." She scowled. "Do you really think my stepmother would allow me to look on a strange man?"

He shrugged. "I don't know the customs here…er, I mean…I really need to get some clothes on…without you watching." He tilted his head.

She sighed. "Very well. We'll speak later."

He nodded, then scowled when she hesitated. "Amanda, please…"

She didn't move. He liked her blue-eyed gaze drifting over him but knew if one of her relatives found her eyeing him like this, there'd be hell to pay.

"I'm going." She gently closed the door.

He still held the undergarment and considered slipping it beneath the sheet but she wouldn't dare return. He hoped.

The last thing he needed was for her parents to think he was trying to seduce their daughter.

Chapter Seven

Amanda tossed, waking in a sweat. *A dream*. She sat up in bed trying to recall what the dream had been about. Erin was there and her father, but they were in a strange world, the likes of which she'd never seen. Erin had taken her and her father to the future.

She closed her eyes, trying to recall as much as she could of the images. Carriages raced down smooth roads at high speeds with no horses or mules to pull them. Faces peered from glass window panes as vehicles flew by at fantastic speeds. Buildings so tall, Amanda imagined they'd reach straight to Heaven. And when she looked up, machines flew overhead, higher than the birds.

People walked by in all types of garb. Many of the women wore trousers or scandalously short skirts. Men strolled by in various stages of undress as well. People raced past on smooth, paved areas, many holding small flat boxes and speaking into them. A group stood in line waiting to enter a large carriage. Again no horses. Smoke spewed from the rear of the vehicle as it angled away from the curb.

Amanda turned as a male voice caught her attention. Jack! He spoke into one of the boxes, then raised his gaze to her. The shirt he wore resembled an undergarment, but was a deep red. His trousers, a denim material, stayed up without braces.

"Amanda." He held out his hand. "I've got so much to show you."

She glanced at her parents, who nodded. Taking his hand, she waved her other arm. "Is this the future?"

Jack laughed. "It's where I live, but to me it's the present."

She glanced at Erin. Her father held her stepmother in his embrace. Erin's wistful gaze drifted over Amanda and Jack.

"It's time to go, Amanda," she said.

"No. Mother, Father, I want to stay here…with Jack."

Jack's arms tightened around her. "Isn't there a way she can stay with me?"

"This is the only way." Erin held up a brooch. "But not yet. She has to come home with us."

Amanda's pulse quickened as she stared at the brooch. Erin had shown her this very brooch, with her father's chocolate-brown hair, when Amanda was a small child. He'd given it to Erin when he was in the war.

"Mother, please, show me how to stay here with Jack," Amanda cried.

Erin shook her head. Her father gazed at her, then lifted his arm in a beckoning gesture.

Jack's arms tightened around her. "I'll never let you go," he gasped. But his grip dissolved.

"No!" Amanda cried. Her hands twisted in her nightgown. She sat alone on her bed. Her body heated as she tried to decipher what had just happened.

Had she wakened from a dream and had a vision, or had it all been part of the dream?

No matter what, she had to find the brooch. It

might be the only way for her to see the future with Jack.

****

Erin brought Jack breakfast. "I'm tired of lying around," he told her as she set down his tray. "I'd like to get out of this room. I'm going stir crazy."

"Can't say as I blame you, Jack. You've been cooped up here for days. I see you found your clothes." She pointed to one corner of the room. "Your boots are over there."

"Thanks." Jack fingered the rough clothing he'd donned, wishing he had a T-shirt or jeans to put on. He didn't relish walking around in these archaic things.

Erin stood and smoothed out her skirts. "I'll send someone up to bring you down in a few minutes." She stepped to the dresser and rifled through a drawer, returning with a pair of socks. "But be careful what you say. My husband knows about my other life, but others might be confused if you make mention to the future. Or use modern slang expressions."

"I understand." Jack's gaze followed her as she left the room and closed the door behind her. He wondered who she'd send up after him. He hoped it would be Amanda, but likely it would be her son or Mrs. O'Leary.

He hastily pulled on the woolen socks and lifted the suspenders, attached to the waistband of the loose trousers he wore, slipping them over his shoulders. Without the suspenders, the pants would slide down as he walked. But at least the clothes weren't that uncomfortable. He pulled on the boots. They were old and worn. The man he inhabited seemed to be a poor, working class stiff. Just his luck.

He stepped to the mirror atop the dresser and studied his face. His cheeks looked a bit thinner, but likely that was due to his injury and confinement. He hadn't exactly been eating on a regular basis. He'd been unconscious for at least a day and mostly slept through the next few days. He rubbed his hand along his cheek. He needed a shave, but otherwise, he didn't see much difference in his appearance, except for a shaggier haircut.

If he was in a body of someone from the past, he must be an ancestor. Erin believed she'd lived in this century. Was he reliving his former life? Who had he been in this time period?

Suddenly, he was hungry to learn all he could.

A knock at the door startled him. He took one last glance in the mirror, then stepped toward the door.

Amanda stood outside, a blush coloring her cheeks. He longed to reach up and stroke her ivory skin. He imagined it would feel like flower petals. "Mother sent me up to fetch you. Do you think you can manage the stairs?"

Jack grinned. "With your help, Amanda, I can manage anything."

She bit her lip. "I'll take you to the top of the stairs. You can hold onto the rail, and I'll hold your other arm to be sure you don't fall."

"Very courageous of you." He grinned again.

Her eyes widened. "You're making fun of me."

"Oh, no. I'm sure you're very strong and competent, it's just…"

"Just what?" She scowled.

"If I fall, I'm sure we'll both end up in a heap at the bottom of the stairs."

She pursed her lips and held out her hand to him. Her grip was firm, but also soft and warm. Although he tried to focus on walking, his mind raced with the intoxicating scent drifting from her and how smooth the skin of her face appeared. Her figure in the flowing gown proved a bit of a mystery. Did they all wear corsets in this century? He didn't dare probe her waistline to find out.

At the top of the staircase, she halted, moving his hand to the flat top of the post. He glanced down the stairs. Uncarpeted and steep looking, but not unlike the old homes he refurbished.

Her red-gold lashes brushed her cheek, then her gaze rose to meet his. "You seem to have regained your balance. Can you manage the stairs?"

He gulped, trying to shift his brain to the task at hand. "Sure I can."

"Hold the railing. I'll be right on your other side." She smiled. "Take it slow."

He nodded. Gripping the polished wood banister, he took one step, then another. He felt a bit wobbly, but with Amanda supporting his other side, was sure he wouldn't fall and make an ass of himself on the narrow staircase. Amanda pressed against the wall on one side and him on the other. Her close proximity caused his breath to hitch. Once they'd reached the bottom, he blew out a sigh of relief.

"Told you I could do it," he said.

He caught her answering grin. "You are quite arrogant about your abilities, Mr. Lawton."

"Jack," he corrected.

At her frown, he added, "Even your stepmom calls me Jack."

Her brows lifted.

Voices from the hall caught Jack's attention. One was male, the other sounded like Erin.

"Oh, no," Amanda said.

"What is it?" Jack's pulse sped up.

"It sounds like…"

The parlor doors stood open. "I must see Amanda now." The male voice sounded insistent.

"She's upstairs caring for our guest." Erin's face appeared at the open door. She waved her arm in a gesture of warning.

Amanda sighed. "It's my boss."

"Your boss?" Jack glanced from Amanda to Erin. "Are you in trouble or something?"

Erin spread her hands. "He insisted on calling on you even though I told him…"

A man pushed past her into the hall. He wore a brown coat, a thin black tie, and a round brimmed hat clutched in his hand. A thin mustache was the only facial hair on his pale face. "Amanda?" His glare took in her and Jack. "This is the invalid you've been caring for?"

Jack stepped forward, but Amanda threw out her arm to warn him back.

"What is your name, sir, and how did you get here?" The man scowled.

"Randolph, he's our guest." She glanced at Jack. "He was hit on the head and lost his memory." She crossed her arms over her chest in a challenging gesture.

Jack inhaled, figuring he'd better just play along.

Randolph turned to face Erin. "You told me this man was a relative."

She bit her lip.

"She told you that to protect my respectability," Amanda said. "He was hurt and unconscious. What would you have us do?" She spread her arms.

Randolph stepped closer, his gaze focusing on Jack. "He's dressed as a common workman." He sniffed. "Wherever did you find him?"

"You don't have to talk about me as if I wasn't here." Jack faced Randolph. "I can speak for myself."

"But if you've lost your memory, as these ladies claim…" Randolph smirked.

Jack lifted a hand to probe the back of his head. "I can assure you the beam that flattened me caused memory loss. When I woke, I didn't know where I was or who I was."

Amanda turned her head to shoot him a warning glance. He knew better than to say too much to this guy.

He possessively brushed his hand over her arm. "If Amanda hadn't found me, I might've died right there."

"Amanda?" Randolph's face turned red. "He's calling you by your Christian name?"

Amanda bit her lip, but nodded. "It was easier, seeing as we're caring for him."

"And what do you call him?" Randolph sneered.

"She calls me Jack as does her stepmother." He gestured toward Erin.

Randolph withdrew a handkerchief from his vest pocket and pressed it to his nose as if to ward off a bad smell. "Well…it looks as if you're up and about now. I take it you'll be returning to your home."

Erin stepped forward. "He doesn't remember where he lives. We're allowing him to stay until he does."

"But this is highly improper, madam." Randolph pinned Amanda with a scowl, then turned his attention back to her mother. "Your daughter is young and unmarried and this man is…is…"

Jack stepped to within an inch of the simpering man's face. He'd had all he could take of his accusations. "Is what?"

Amanda grasped Jack's arm and gently pulled him back. "I think I should speak to Randolph alone."

"And I think you shouldn't." He held her arm to prevent her from leaving his side.

"Jack, please." Her gaze held his. "I can take care of myself."

Erin nodded. "They'll be in the parlor." She stepped to Jack's side and grasped his arm. "We'll go to the kitchen. I'm sure Mrs. O'Leary has something for you to eat."

Jack glanced at Amanda, then Randolph.

Erin tilted her head toward the hall. "She'll be fine." She patted his forearm.

"Okay," he relented. "If you're sure."

Amanda nodded. "Go on. I'll be out shortly."

He allowed Erin to lead him to a doorway down the hall. When she pushed the door open, delicious aromas drew his interest. He turned back once, but she led him into the room.

"It'll be all right, Jack."

But he wished he'd had the chance to flatten the pompous bastard. In time, maybe he would.

Chapter Eight

Once Randolph had taken his leave and Jack had gone upstairs for a nap, Amanda decided she needed to confront her stepmother and find out what the devil was going on between her and Jack. And how much did her father know?

Well, she damned well planned to find out.

Erin sat alone in the parlor, a notebook perched on her lap. Her gaze wandered to Amanda, while she chewed absently on the end of a pencil.

"Mother." Amanda stepped into the room and closed the doors behind her. "I need to speak with you."

Erin set her pad and pencil on the small end table and sat up straighter, twisting in Amanda's direction. "What is it, dear?"

Amanda perched on the chair beside Erin. "I want to talk to you about Jack…and also Randolph."

"Jack?" Erin's brows rose. "Is he all right?"

"He's fine." Amanda sighed, folding her hands in her lap. "I don't think Randolph much likes Jack staying with us."

Erin leaned forward. "Does his opinion bother you?"

"I really don't care what Randolph thinks."

"I see."

"Mother, I know you don't like Randolph, but he's the most suitable man for me in town right now. At least Father thinks so. He's also provided me with a job that I love."

"I know." Erin rose and paced before the fireplace. "But I'd hoped you wouldn't allow him to sway your affections. I don't believe he's the right man for you."

"Father wouldn't agree." Amanda frowned.

"Your father is a man of his time…" Erin turned away.

Amanda rose. "What do you mean?"

"Ah…" Erin planted a hand on her hip and turned to face Amanda. "He's just old-fashioned in his thinking, not forward thinking like…"

"Like you?"

Erin nodded.

"Mother, you always told me Father was a forward thinking man. It's why you fell in love with him."

"Guess I worded that wrong." Erin bit her lip.

Amanda fisted her hands and propped them on her hips. "I only agreed to allow Randolph to court me as a means to an end. But if he's my only opportunity for marriage and family, I don't have much of a choice." She sucked on her lower lip. "Jack is so different than any man I've ever met."

"He's a working class man, dear. How many of them do you even speak to?"

"You'd be surprised." Amanda rounded on her stepmother. "I think a man who works with his hands is incredibly appealing."

Erin smiled. "You and me both."

"But Father's a banker." Amanda protested.

"When I met him, he was a soldier."

"An officer."

"A man who rode horses, lived in an army camp,

marched out to face enemy soldiers..." Erin sighed.

"I understand, Mother. If he'd been a banker when you first met him, you'd likely have never given him the time of day."

"When you're attracted to a man..." Erin crossed her arms over her bodice. "...you feel tingly when he's near." She gazed at Amanda. "When that happens, you'll know he's the man for you."

"Is this how you felt when you first met Father?" Amanda studied her stepmother's face.

She nodded. "But he did frighten me at first."

Amanda hugged herself. "Jack excites me. I want to help him, but something about him scares me."

"He's harmless. Just a lost soul is all." Erin glanced away.

Footsteps in the hall drew Amanda's attention. The door opened, revealing her father.

"Here you two are." He stepped into the room. "The house seemed deserted when I arrived."

Erin glanced toward the clock on the mantel. "Mrs. O'Leary mustn't have started supper yet. Is Billy with you?"

"No, I left early. Wanted to be sure everything's all right here?"

"Why wouldn't it be?" Amanda eyed her father.

"Ah, just overthinking on my part, I suppose."

Erin stepped toward her husband, fingering his collar. "It's no matter. Any excuse to spend more time with you is to my liking."

"I think I'll be checking on Jack." Amanda edged around her parents wanting to give them privacy.

"Bring him down if he's up to it," Erin said. "I'm sure he's tired of being cooped up in Billy's room. You could take him out into the garden."

"I will." Amanda left the parlor and ascended the stairs. Her pulse raced in anticipation of seeing Jack. She recalled her stepmother's description of how Amanda would know when she found the right man.

****

Jack stood by the window gazing over the street below. His thoughts were in a jumble over his predicament. How the hell was he going to get home? Was it even possible?

And if he could, what about Amanda? The click of footsteps in the hall drew his attention from the window. A soft rap sounded.

"Come in. I'm decent," he called.

The door opened, and Amanda slipped into the room, a grin spreading across her face.

"My mother suggested I take you outside…if you're feeling up to it." Her full lips twisted.

"Do I?" Adrenaline rushed through his body at the thought of finally escaping the house.

"Well…" Amanda stepped toward him and glanced out the window. "I thought maybe you'd be up for a tour of Mother's garden before supper."

"Great!" He shoved his hands in his pockets. "I'm sick of being cooped up."

"All right, let's go then."

Jack crooked his arm as he'd seen the other men do. Amanda wrapped both her arms around his extended one, her warmth and softness so close. The urge to lean over and kiss her lips overwhelmed him. He had to get a grip on himself. In his own century it might work, but here? He decided he'd better err on the side of caution and follow her lead.

Her scent drifted over him, flowery and sweet. Her smooth forehead a breath from his lips, as she led him out into the hallway.

"Mother and Father are in the parlor, but I don't want to disturb them." She giggled as they reached the top of the stairs. "I think they were on the verge of getting romantic."

Jack smiled, intrigued at the thought. "Your mother is a remarkable woman."

"She is," Amanda agreed. "She's encouraged me to go beyond the boundaries set for proper young ladies. Told me to follow my dreams and live how I want, not what society demands of me."

She held tight to his arm as they eased down the staircase.

"And what does your father have to say?"

"Oh, he's a bit more conservative about how a young lady should behave." At the bottom of the stairs, she lifted her chin, tilting her head. "But he always bows to Mother's wishes. He wouldn't dare try to order her around, like other men do with their wives." She grinned. "Let's go see the garden."

Chapter Nine

Amanda led him through the kitchen to a door that opened to the rear of the house. She stopped on a small porch with three steps leading to a garden. Assorted flowers, shrubs, and neat rows of vegetables took up the space, except for a flagstone path with a stone bench set to the side.

He followed Amanda out onto the path, then stopped and gazed around.

"Are you all right?" Concern creased her face. "You don't feel dizzy or weak, do you?"

He patted his chest. "No. In fact, this is the best I've felt since...well, since before I was conked on the head."

She laughed. The sound caused him to grin. "You think it's funny?"

"No, not at all." She held up her hand. "It's the way you said it, I suspect. Struck me as funny."

Emboldened by her humor, he lifted his hand to the small of her back. Her lashes dipped, then she gazed at him, her tongue flitting out to lick her lower lip.

"Shall we sit?" she asked.

"Sounds good." He waved his other arm for her to precede him down the path.

They stopped by the bench. She gathered her skirts and settled onto the stone surface. He sat beside her, not sure what to do next.

"Just breathe it all in," she said.

He took a deep breath, taking in the assorted aromas. It felt good to be outdoors.

After a few moments of awkward silence, Amanda cleared her throat.

Jack swiveled his head to gaze down at her. A red-gold strand of hair had come loose from her bun and dangled over her cheek. He longed to reach out and brush it back but held himself in check.

She lifted a hand and pushed the strand back into her bun, then gazed up at him, biting her lip.

"You should leave it loose," he said on impulse.

Her eyes widened. "I beg your pardon?"

"Your hair is beautiful but would look a lot better hanging loose around your shoulders." In fact, he'd love to see it around her bared shoulders but didn't dare voice the idea.

Although her mouth gaped, a hint of a smile showed in her eyes. "Do ladies in your time wear their hair down outside the bedroom?"

"Yeah, some do." He sat back and scowled, realizing she'd tricked him.

"Jack, it's all right. I know you don't come from here. You're from the time where my stepmother came from."

Jack stiffened. "I don't think we should be talking about this."

"Please." She grasped his hand and held it between her own. "I've heard stories about your time ever since I was a small girl. I've always dreamed of going there. Mother told me all about the flying machines and great ships that fly off into space. The moon even! Just like in a Jules Verne novel." She dropped his hand and clasped hers together. "You have to take me there. Show me all of it."

"Amanda." Jack sighed. "I'm not even sure how I got here, or if I can ever go back."

Her gaze dropped to the path. "I so want to go."

"Believe me…" Jack raised his hand. "If I knew how to do it, I'd take you."

"You would?" Her gaze rose to his.

He shrugged. "I don't know how."

"But you would take me?"

He nodded, unsure of what else to say.

"There might be a way, but I have to get hold of my stepmother's brooch."

"A brooch?" Jack frowned. "What does a brooch have to do with anything?"

Amanda leaned forward. "I think this brooch is what sent my stepmother back in time, then returned her." She caught his gaze and shrugged. "It's worth a try."

"How does it work?"

"I'm not sure." She shook her head.

"Your stepmother told me she returned to the future after being shot." He brushed a hand over his chest. "I don't like that idea much."

"There must be another way." She lifted a hand and laid it atop his. "I don't like the idea of you being shot either."

Jack held his breath. Her fingers rested over his heart. He grasped her hand, entwining their fingers.

Her face colored. "We should be getting inside. It must be near time for supper."

"Wait." Jack grasped her wrist to keep her from pulling away. "What about this Randolph? How do you feel about him?"

"I-I'm not sure. My stepmother says he's not right for me." She scowled.

"Because he's old-fashioned?" Jack guessed.

She lifted her gaze to his. "Why do you say that?"

"It's what your stepmother told me. Why she doesn't want you to marry him."

Amanda smiled. "Yes. He's boorish and has outdated ideas. He believes a woman is only useful when she's tending to her home, man, and children."

"But you work for him."

"It's a great opportunity, such that it is." She shrugged. "What about the women of your time?"

"They can do any type of job they want and are qualified for." He grinned. "They even get to fly into space with the men."

Amanda gasped. "You can't be serious." She lifted both hands to her mouth. "What a wonderful place to live!" She dropped her gaze and twisted her hands in her skirts. "But I'm sure with all those modern women to choose from, you'd have no interest in an old-fashioned girl like me."

"Amanda…" Jack took both her hands in his. "I've never met anyone like you. When I first saw your photo—"

"My photo?" She frowned. "Where did you see it?"

"It was in the house where you found me, but in the future. It was hanging on the wall at the bottom of the stairs."

"In the house Randolph is building?" Her lower lip trembled.

Jack leaned forward, unable to stop himself, and lightly brushed his lips over hers. She tasted sweet, like cinnamon and sugar.

She reared back, her lips in a firm line, but then opened, as he enfolded her pliant body in his arms. He stroked his hands around her back and pulled her as close as possible. Her heart beat swiftly, like a delicate, caged bird.

The kiss rocked him to his core. Although he'd dreamed of kissing those lush lips, the reality was so much better. An ache formed in his chest at the thought of going home and never seeing her again.

He finally released her. Her eyes looked a bit glazed, her lips swollen and her hair mussed. He bit his lip, wondering what reception they'd get at supper.

****

Amanda's knees weakened as a thrill raced through her body. No man had ever kissed her like that. Of course, she hadn't had much opportunity with other men. And had never allowed Randolph to get so close.

She gazed into Jack's eyes. His lips twisted into an adorable half-smile, his eyes bright, face flushed. Had he felt the same thing she had?

"Are you okay, Amanda?" His smile turned down into a frown.

"I-I think so." She touched her lips, the sensation of his pressed against hers still with her. She was also very aware of his male scent. If she didn't fear someone would discover them, she'd fling her arms around him for another round of kisses.

"Guess we better go inside." He stood.

She nodded, not trusting herself to speak. He tottered a bit, so she grasped his arm to steady him.

He patted her hand and stepped toward the porch steps. Her breath caught at the warmth radiating from this man. When she first met him, he'd been injured, a partial invalid. Now, even though he wasn't yet fully recovered, she sensed the power in his body. He was a working man, used to wielding heavy tools.

His calloused palms on her body thrilled her. Her face flamed. She had to calm her reaction before they stepped inside.

He led her up the steps onto the porch, then lifted her chin for a brief, sweet kiss. She licked her lips and smiled.

"You wouldn't take such liberties if my father was watching."

He glanced toward the window. "You think he is?"

She laughed, a light, tinkling sound. "You'd better hope not."

He grinned. "He could be in there right now, loading his shotgun."

"He won't force you to marry me, Jack. Not over a kiss." She gathered her skirts as he reached for the doorknob.

"Comforting to know, but…"

"But what?"

His lips found hers again. "If that's what it takes to let me keep kissing you, it's not so bad."

She swatted at him. "I suspect you're teasing me. Let's get in to supper before my stepmother comes looking for us."

Jack opened the door for her and followed her down the hall. Even if no one had been watching from the window, they'd surely get the gist of what mischief they'd been up to by looking at their faces.

****

Hours later, Jack awoke from a sound sleep. His

dreams had been occupied with Amanda. All through supper, he'd sat studying her face. The black and white photo he'd seen in present time in no way did her justice. She looked like a delicate china doll but was full of spirit. The idea of Randolph—even though he barely knew the man—kissing or even touching her, set his teeth on edge.

The problem was, he didn't belong here and had to find a way back to his own time. But if he could, how could he take Amanda with him? And if he couldn't, how could he leave her?

Now, he understood why her stepmother chose to return to this backward time.

Jack dressed, brushed his unruly hair, and ran a hand over his growing beard. He'd entertained the idea of shaving, until Erin brought him a mug with shaving cream and a straight edged razor. The real fear of accidentally slicing his jugular, kept him from giving it a try, even though Erin offered to help.

The idea of Amanda's stepmother assisting him with such an intimate act didn't hold much appeal. He told her he'd wait a few more days to decide.

And maybe, while in this century, he should allow his beard to grow in order to blend in. The men he'd seen since arriving here, all had some type of facial hair, be it a full beard, a mustache, or a combination. Quite possibly, he'd be more attractive to Amanda with hair on his face.

After a quick glance in the mirror, he left his room and descended the stairs. The parlor door stood open and movement inside sent him to the doorway to investigate.

Amanda stood by the window pulling open the

heavy drapes in the small room. She turned, her lips parting in a wide smile when she caught sight of him standing in the doorway.

"Jack!" Her hand rose to her lips. "You look so…"

When she hesitated, he frowned. "So what?" He brushed a hand over his hair, expecting a strand to be sticking straight up. "What's wrong?"

She shook her head. "Nothing at all." She spread her arms. "It's just you look so…so…dashing."

He grinned. "And you look absolutely beautiful this morning."

She giggled and sank into a mock curtsey, spreading out the folds of her voluminous gown. "Why, thank you very much, sir."

He lifted his arm. "Shall we go in to breakfast?"

"Well…" She stepped close and lowered her voice. "I was thinking about skipping breakfast and going to the house." Her gaze met his. "Unless you're hungry."

He patted his stomach. "I kind of am, but if you think this is important…"

She turned toward one of the tables and lifted a folded napkin. "I sneaked a couple of rolls from the kitchen when Mrs. O'Leary was busy at the stove. These should do us for a bit."

"Okay." Jack nodded. "But won't there be workers at the house this time of day?"

"I think we might be able to get there ahead of them and sneak inside."

The aroma of fresh baked bread caused Jack's mouth to water. Amanda slipped him a roll, and he took a bite. "Mmmm. Mrs. O'Leary's a great cook."

Amanda tucked her roll into a pocket of her skirt and lifted a black felt hat from the rack by the door. She pinned it in place and grasped Jack's arm.

"C'mon, before anyone sees us and asks questions."

Jack strolled with Amanda on his arm along tree-lined streets with rows of attached brick homes. In this part of town, most of these homes still stood in his own time. But with the newness of the buildings, the landscape appeared alien.

She led him about four blocks, past storefronts, obviously the business section. She pointed out a detached building on the corner, also brick, with a large glass front. "I work there, Jack. I'm a writer for the town paper." She pointed to a sign in the corner of the window by the glass door.

In fancy lettering, it read: *The Carver Weekly*. As they drew near, Jack read smaller lettering proclaiming the name of the owner, Theodore Carver and the chief editor, Randolph Norwood.

"Norwood." Jack grimaced. "You think he's in there?"

Amanda pulled him aside. "I hope so." She glanced up and down the block. "If he's here, he won't be at the house. And I don't want to run into him right now. I don't have to be at work for another hour."

"Okay, then let's get moving."

She nodded and motioned farther down the block. "We have to go another two blocks before we arrive at the house."

Jack squinted, trying to picture this section of town in his time. He'd driven here by car and wasn't sure of his bearings yet. In the future, this section was a bit run down in places, but in a state of rejuvenation. He'd have loved to buy and renovate the house.

At the end of the block, Amanda pointed toward a lot with two homes under construction. She lifted her skirts and strode toward the street. A horse pulling a carriage cantered past.

Amanda turned toward Jack. "The second one's where I found you that night."

He bit his lip. Several homes occupied this block in his time. His brain had been in a fog when Amanda brought him to her home, so he wasn't sure.

He grasped her arm. "Let's go see."

They crossed the narrow street, striding past the first house. Two workmen stood outside smoking small cigars. They eyed Jack and Amanda, then returned to their conversation.

"What if there are workmen at Randolph's house?" Jack asked.

Amanda shrugged. "We take a look anyway, at least from the outside. Then come back later tonight."

Jack nodded. He stopped before the house staring up the path that led to the porch and front door. A mound of dirt stood on each side of the flagstone path. Jack recalled Mrs. Grayson's garden surrounded by a black wrought iron fence. A gate opened from the sidewalk into the path. This had to be the house.

She tightened her grip on his arm. "Jack, I don't see any workmen about."

"Me either." He stepped away from the path toward the side of the house. She followed.

"Either they're off today, or they haven't gotten here yet," he said.

Amanda's gaze scanned the unpainted, wood exterior. "I don't see anyone through the windows either. This is how it was when I found you. No one was here."

"You're sure Randolph won't show up? I can bluff my way past workmen, but—"

"I'm sure, Jack. He'd be at the office this time of morning. He always is."

Jack sucked on his inner cheeks, trying to decide. This house might be the only way for him to get home. He had to get inside.

He led Amanda back to the path. After scanning both ends of the street and noting no one paid them any attention, he led her onto the porch. The porch and door hadn't yet been painted, but the doorknob was in place.

"Amanda, I'm sure this door will be locked, if the workers aren't here yet."

She shook her head, sending a tendril of curled hair bouncing against her cheek. "It wasn't the morning I found you. Randolph wanted to take me to dinner, then show me the house. I declined but decided to get up early the next day and take a look by myself. The door was closed but not locked."

"Okay." Jack tilted his head and reached for the knob. The door opened inward.

Amanda flashed him a grin. "I told you."

He glanced behind them. "Let's get inside before anyone sees us and hope no one's standing inside with a shotgun aimed in our direction."

Amanda huffed a protest, but he noted her hand clamped around his upper arm as he led her in. After a quick scan, he gently closed the door, hoping they hadn't walked into a trap.

The house looked as it had when Amanda had helped him out. He crept through the unfinished foyer, glancing into the room that would become the parlor.

The empty room relaxed him a bit. But he had to be sure the house was deserted.

"I should check the kitchen before we head upstairs." He turned toward Amanda. "You stay here. Give a yell if you see or hear anyone."

She nodded. "Be careful."

He crept toward the back of the house. The layout was familiar from the time he'd spent here with Mrs. Grayson. But everything was fresh and new, down to the heady scent of fresh cut wood. The big room stood empty. He stepped inside but took care not to let his boots echo on the bare wood floor.

Convinced no one lurked in any of the corners ready to dive out at him, Jack backtracked to the foyer just outside the parlor. Amanda stood at the base of the staircase, glancing upward.

Jack stepped to her side. "This is the spot where your picture was hanging." He pointed to the wall at eye level above the bottom step.

"Here?" She frowned.

"The young woman in the photo looked remarkably like you and hung right there. I noticed it was still up after the house had been emptied out. For some reason, the new owner hadn't taken the picture down." Jack shook his head. "I swear, it looked exactly like you, right down to the hairstyle and clothing."

Amanda bit her lip. "Maybe the photo is what sent you here. To me."

Jack grinned. "Nice theory. But how am I supposed to get back?"

She shrugged, her gaze locked on his. "We'd better get upstairs before someone comes."

"I'll go first." Jack crept up the stairs, glancing

behind him every few steps to be sure Amanda followed. His heart thudded at the eerie quiet on the upper floor. No footsteps echoed on the uncarpeted surfaces. For sure, he and Amanda's movements would have drawn attention from anyone inside the house.

Close to the top of the staircase, he climbed more swiftly, taking Amanda's hand to draw her with him. He scanned the hall, then pulled her along to another room not yet fitted with a door. Sunlight shimmered through.

"This is the room." He glanced at Amanda.

She nodded. "Yes. I found you here."

He took a deep breath and stepped into the bright room, adorned only with tools and sawhorses. No sign of any workmen. He breathed a sigh of relief.

Amanda slipped from behind him, pointing to a spot on the floor, where a large beam lay. Jack stepped toward the spot, noting blood on the unfinished wood.

"You were right there."

He took her hand. "It's hard to remember. I did sneak into this house for a last look, but it was old, decrepit. When I came into this room, it was empty, like this, except the floorboards were rotted and loose in spots. I was afraid I'd fall through."

"Then what happened?" Amanda breathed.

Her mouth gaped as she gazed around the room, her eyes bright, breath quick and shallow.

"You okay?" He searched her face.

"Oh, Jack, this is so exciting." Her eyes widened. "This room might be a doorway to the future."

"Or the past," he agreed.

She gasped with delight and pulled him close, planting a kiss on his cheek. "What if we could stand right here in this spot, close our eyes, and transport to the future?"

"It would be nice." Jack rubbed the sore spot on the back of his head. "But I don't know if it would work without us being knocked unconscious."

"Oh." Amanda bit her lip. "What did my mother tell you about her travel back and forth?"

"She said she'd come back after losing consciousness in a car accident. Then went forward after being shot."

Amanda sighed. "Doesn't sound too promising." She spun toward the window that looked over the rear yard. Trees and shrubs covered the landscape.

Jack remembered houses behind these when he visited with Mrs. Grayson. "I don't know. As much as I want to go home, I really don't want to get hit with another beam." He held Amanda's gaze. "Don't think you want to either."

Her scent and warmth so close beside him sent all thoughts of the future flying out the window. On impulse, he leaned toward her, his lips a breath away from hers.

Her eyelids flew upward, gaze focused on his mouth. She blew out a breathy sigh, her eyes closing.

He pressed his lips gently over hers, his tongue gliding out to pry her lips apart. She opened to him, lifting her arms to circle his neck.

He slid his hands around her back, pulling her close. His breath mingled with her sweetness as his senses spiraled. He wanted this woman badly. Images rose behind his closed eyelids of her photo, waking up to her face above him, the time he'd spent with her at her parents' house.

She let out a small gasp, forcing him back to reality.

Footsteps thudded across the floor below them.

"Oh, shit!" Jack said.

Amanda backed away and glanced toward the doorway. "What should we do, Jack?"

He swallowed. "Stay quiet, for now. I'll figure some way out."

Amanda stood still, fists pressed against her mouth.

Jack sucked his lower lip, trying to figure a way out of this mess. He strained his ears for any sounds. Male voices drifted toward them from downstairs.

Holy shit! He'd have to take Amanda by the hand and try to make a run for it.

He shuffled toward the door, trying not to draw the men's attention. Pausing in the doorway, he glanced toward the stairs. They'd have to time it right.

Amanda stood still, her eyes wide. He motioned her to his side but made a shushing sound, pointing to her feet.

She nodded and shuffled toward him, her arm reaching out.

He drew in a breath to calm himself, trying to imagine the worst that would happen. So a couple of disgruntled workmen cursed them out. They'd have no idea who the couple was and think they'd come inside to make out. He grinned at the idea.

"Come," he whispered and reached for Amanda's outstretched hand. She placed her hand in his, drawing in a strained breath.

He nodded toward the stairs. "Follow me down, but don't stop for anything. Understand?"

Her eyes widened, but she nodded.

"Okay, one…two…"

"Three." A rough male voice sounded from below.

Jack glanced toward the stairs where a heavily bearded, round face peered at them from the base of the steps. "And what do we have here, then?"

Chapter Ten

Jack glanced at Amanda. She pursed her lips.

"We—I mean, I…" Jack shrugged, hoping the man would think them lovers looking for a private place.

The man, dressed in work clothes, stomped to the top of the stairs and leered at Amanda. He slapped a large hammer against his beefy hand. "Reckon I'll take her to the back room for a little lesson on breaking into buildings that don't belong to you."

Amanda fisted her hands, placing them on her hips. "You will not, sir. We were just leaving. C'mon, Jack." She stepped toward the workman.

His eyes widened on his weather beaten face. "See here, girl."

"I'm no girl." She shoved past him on the narrow staircase, her feet shuffling down the steps. "Jack?" she called out without a backward glance.

Jack didn't move, his gaze shifting from the workman to the hammer.

The man glanced down the stairs at Amanda's hasty retreat and shrugged. "Best do as the lady says."

Jack didn't need a special invitation. He drew in his breath and squeezed past the workman, who didn't give an inch, then raced down the stairs.

He caught up to Amanda at the front door. "You've got a lot of guts for a…"

"A girl?" she finished for him.

"No. A strong and beautiful woman."

She grinned and pulled the door open. Two workmen stood outside, their mouths agape.

"Who the devil are *you*?" The tall, thin one asked.

"Nobody." Jack grasped Amanda's hand. "And we were just leaving."

He led her down the street. Once out of sight of the house and workmen, Amanda doubled over in a fit of giggles.

"You think that was funny?" Jack asked. Although the look on the men's faces was comical, disappointment washed over him at still not knowing how he'd ever get home.

"Oh, Jack." Amanda took a few deep breaths. "I'm sorry. I know how much going home means to you." She lifted a gloved hand to his cheek. "I told you how much I want to go too."

He sighed, catching her hand and lifting it away from his face. "I don't think your parents would agree."

She drew herself up to her full height, her eyes level with Jack's mouth. "I'm an adult woman. What I do is my choice. My stepmother taught me to make my own decisions."

"But if you came with me, they'd never see you again."

She shook her head. "A lot of young women marry and move far away from their homes."

"Yeah, but they can still write home. You won't have that luxury."

"Oh, Jack, we'll figure something out, I swear."

Although Jack hoped for a happy outcome for them both, he was sure it would never be a possibility given the circumstances.

****

Amanda's lips still tingled from the kiss she'd shared with Jack. If Randolph had caught them, there'd be hell to pay. But she thrilled to imagine what more Jack could show her if they had more time by themselves.

As they rounded the corner leading to her home, Amanda glanced down the block and stiffened.

Jack stared at her. "What's wrong?"

"Look." She inclined her head. Randolph stood at her front door.

"What's he doing here?" Jack's muscles tensed beneath her fingers.

"He's likely looking for me."

"You supposed to be at work or something?" Jack's scowl deepened as his gaze locked on Randolph.

Amanda inhaled deeply. "I should have been at the newspaper office over an hour ago. Time got away from me."

"Well, there's nothing to do but get this over with." Jack rubbed the back of her hand as she curled her fingers around his arm. His touch calmed her nerves a bit. He led her toward her house.

Randolph turned in their direction. His eyes widened, then narrowed.

"Amanda, why aren't you at the office? I feared you'd taken ill."

His scowl settled on Jack. Amanda clutched his arm with both hands.

"I-I…" Her face colored.

"I needed Amanda to help me," Jack said.

Amanda stiffened beside him, as her gaze slid from him to Randolph.

"Help you with what?" Randolph demanded.

"Ah…" Jack glanced to Amanda for help.

"He's still having trouble walking and needed some necessities from the mercantile."

Jack nodded, his gaze locked on Randolph's.

Randolph sneered. "You couldn't have fetched the items for him? Or couldn't anyone else in the household have? You do have household help, after all."

"Mrs. O'Leary was busy with breakfast, and my father and brother had to be at work." Amanda's fingers moved up and down Jack's coat sleeve, steadying her.

"As do you," Randolph pointed out.

"I-I'm taking today off. Mother is busy today, and Jack needs me."

Randolph stepped toward them. "Amanda, you should take your position on the paper seriously, not cater to a man's whim." His scowl rested on Jack.

"It's not a whim. He was seriously injured."

Randolph yanked off a glove. "And how, pray tell, did this injury happen?"

"He—"

Jack patted Amanda's hand. She caught his warning glance. The last thing she needed was for Randolph to know they'd been trespassing in his house.

"Amanda, I'm feeling a bit dizzy. If we could go inside?" Jack inclined his head.

She grasped his arm tighter. "Of course. I have to take Jack inside. We'll talk about this later."

Randolph's face reddened. "You won't be in to the office?"

"No, Randolph. Not today." She guided Jack past Randolph and through the front door.

Randolph stood his ground, but finally turned away with a final backward scowl. "I'll expect you in early tomorrow, Amanda."

She didn't answer, closing the door. "Let me get you into the parlor where you can lie down."

Jack raised a hand. "It's all right. I'm fine."

"But you said—" She frowned.

"I wanted to get away from Randolph. He was asking questions we don't want to answer."

She clasped a hand to her mouth, her eyes growing wide.

"We can't tell him you found me in his house," Jack said.

"Of course. I'm so glad you thought of it. Before I see him again, I'll come up with another explanation."

Jack clenched his fist. "I wish you didn't have to work for the pompous ass."

Amanda bit her lip to keep from laughing out loud at his earnestness. "He is that. But I need this job. My hope is to move on to one of the big Philadelphia papers."

Jack frowned. "Does he know this?"

"Amanda!" Erin stepped into the foyer. "Where were you? Randolph was here looking for you. He said you never came to work." She gestured toward the closed door. "He just left."

"I know, Mother. We ran into him when we were coming back."

Erin's gaze shifted from Amanda to Jack. "Coming back from where?"

Jack stepped in front of Amanda. "We went to the house."

Erin's eyes widened. "Was anyone there?"

"Not at first, Mother." Amanda stepped around Jack. "Some workmen arrived after we looked at the room."

"The room where you found Jack?" Erin's gaze fixed on him.

"We did. But I didn't feel anything strange...any vibrations or...whatever sent me here in the first place."

Erin nodded. "You must have had some kind of catalyst." She paced between the parlor door and the base of the stairs. "Did you have anything on your person before you were hit with the beam?"

Jack shook his head. "Nothing out of the ordinary..." He tapped his lip with a fingertip. "Wait a second! I had a photo." His gaze caught Amanda's. "Your photo."

She frowned. "You had it with you?"

Erin grasped Jack's arm. "We have to talk. Alone."

"Mother, whatever you have to say to Jack, you can tell me." Amanda glared at her stepmother.

"No, Amanda. This must be between Jack and me." She nodded at him. "We'll explain everything to you later."

Jack's mouth opened. He glanced toward Amanda, apparently bothered by her stepmother's dismissal.

"Can I speak to Amanda for a second?" Jack asked Erin.

She frowned, but nodded. "I'll be waiting outside your room. Make it quick." With a final glance at Amanda, Erin left the parlor.

Jack grasped Amanda's shoulder. "I don't know why she doesn't want you there, but—trust me—I'll tell you everything she said later."

Amanda crossed her arms over her chest. "She

thinks she can keep me in the dark."

Jack shook his head. "I think she's trying to protect you."

"From what?" She threw up her arms. "I already know where you came from."

"Let me see what she wants to tell me, then I'll find you." He grasped her hand. "I love you, Amanda, and I won't do anything without consulting you first."

She drew in a deep breath. "If my stepmother's found a way to send you back, she won't allow me to go with you."

"We're getting ahead of ourselves." Jack lifted a palm. "I may have to spend the rest of my life here." He grinned. "Would that be so bad?"

Amanda sighed. The prospect of Jack staying here, instead of the other way around had occurred to her. "I suppose not." Her gaze lifted to his.

"I didn't think so." He glanced toward the open parlor door. "I'll be right back. Wait for me here."

She nodded and gathered her skirts taking a seat on the settee. She'd wait for now.

****

Erin stood outside Jack's closed door. She motioned him to silence.

He pushed the door open and allowed her to precede him, then stepped in, checking to be sure no other household member saw them before shutting the door.

"Amanda's upset that you didn't include her."

Erin pursed her lips and folded her arms across her chest. "I know. I hate to leave her in the dark, but Will and I agreed we'd raise her without telling her the whole story of where I'd come from."

Jack motioned Erin to sit in the chair by the window. He sat on the bed.

"She said you'd told her stories about the future."

Erin waved a hand. "That's all they were supposed to be. Stories to entertain a young girl. I am a writer, after all."

"I understand. Knowing where you came from, she'd talk to other people. Raise suspicions about you."

"Yes." Erin quirked a brow. "I'm thought of as a bit eccentric and forward thinking, nothing more. That's how we plan to keep it. I can't pretend to be what I'm not." She held Jack's gaze.

"But you do think there's a way to send me back?"

"I can't say for sure, but since you told me about the photo…"

Jack's face heated. "I don't have the photo. It was in the pocket of my sweat jacket. The one I was wearing in the present before I was hit by the beam." He sighed. "When Amanda found me I was wearing those old workmen's clothes."

Erin nodded. "Exactly what happened to me. I had the brooch in my car when it crashed, but woke up in the army camp wearing a long gown. They'd taken me to the hospital tent." Her lips curved up a bit. "And my hair had grown long." She fingered the tendrils that had slipped from her knot.

"No shit!" Jack's face heated. "Sorry."

She smiled. "No harm done." Raising a finger, she added, "But watch it around Amanda. When she was little, I taught her some words that well…got me into a bit of trouble."

"I bet." Jack crossed his arms and hunched over his thighs. "How'd you end up in the hospital tent? Did you just appear there?"

She shook her head. "The way it was told to me, I'd fallen off a horse, and it was Will, my husband, who brought me to the tent. He and the doctor were there when I woke up." She laughed. "I thought I was at a Civil War reenactment."

"But you were on a horse?"

"Well, not me exactly, but my former self who'd lived during the Civil War."

Jack frowned. "It's hard to make sense of it." He clenched his hand. "I woke up in the very house I was in before I moved through time."

"You said the photo of Amanda was in the house." Erin stood and paced the room.

"Yeah. So, is that why the house sent me here?"

Erin turned and eyed him. "The house? Interesting theory. The house belongs to Randolph." She paced again and shook her head. "And you woke up in workman's clothes." She snapped her fingers. "You must have lived before as a workman and the beam hit him—I mean your former self—just as the beam hit you in the present."

Jack scratched his head. "Sort of makes sense. But who was I in this time?"

"We should be able to find out. Someone may be looking for you right now."

"Doesn't exactly make me feel better."

Erin paced again. "But Amanda's photo was hanging in the house." She seemed to be speaking to herself.

Jack's gaze followed her motions. Her finger tapped her lips, then she turned to face him.

"Does it mean Amanda marries Randolph?"

Jack's blood heated. He stood. "I sure hope not."

Erin stepped to the window and gazed out. "I'm trying like hell to prevent the bastard from getting his hooks into Amanda. I raised her to be her own woman, and from what I've seen of Randolph, the man's a control freak, like a lot of men in this century."

"But not your husband."

Erin turned to face Jack and smiled. "No. It's what attracted me to him in the first place." She waved a hand. "Oh, he acted the hard-assed officer at first, but I quickly saw through him to find a Southern gentleman who'd been hurt badly." She held Jack's gaze. "By the death of his first wife, Amanda's mother."

"So, you came to his aid as he did yours." Jack grinned.

She sighed. "We helped each other until I found myself back home. But I couldn't go back to my old life without him.

"Once I returned, I decided then and there I could never leave him, even for the future conveniences and luxuries I still miss. What I wouldn't give for a cheese pizza!" She lifted a finger. "But being with Will makes the sacrifice worthwhile. I can't live without him."

"I sort of feel the same about Amanda…from the first moment I woke and saw her face. I even dreamed about her before I came here."

Erin's smile wilted into a frown. "Jack, if I can find a way to send you home, what about Amanda?"

"If it's possible to send me home, I'd like to take her with me."

Erin stepped to the chair and plopped down, her face drained of color.

"Are you okay?" Jack strode to her side.

"I-I don't think it's possible, Jack. From what I believe one can only move back into the past to a former life. You have to have another life to inhabit, and Amanda doesn't have one in the future. Her father would never allow her to try it, anyway."

"And what about you?" Jack focused on her face, afraid of her answer.

She shook her head. "I can't allow Amanda to go to the future. We'd never see her again." She wrinkled her brow, her eyes dull.

"But I can't go without her. She wants to go."

Erin nodded. "Of course she'd want to go, but she doesn't understand that it means leaving her family and everything she knows forever."

Jack's pulse raced out of control at the idea of leaving Amanda and never seeing her again. "I promised Amanda I'd at least try to take her with me."

"Jack, you must promise me if I help you, you won't attempt to take Amanda back. I must insist on this. You have to discourage her, even if it means telling her you don't want her."

Jack swallowed, but nodded. What right did he have to deprive this woman and her husband of their daughter? He'd have to break the news to Amanda and hope she believed him.

Chapter Eleven

Amanda paced the length of her room. What was taking Jack so long? She'd waited in the parlor, but her father and brother arrived and took up residence there while waiting for Mrs. O'Leary to prepare supper.

She quickly left to avoid any questions her father had about her stepmother and Jack. She could hardly tell them they were together in his room discussing…well, whatever she'd wanted to talk to him about. Amanda ached to know and couldn't even engage in polite conversation about their day at the bank.

So, she'd begged off saying she had to work on a story, and retreated to her room. Jack's door was closed, and she didn't dare try eavesdropping again. She'd vowed to wait until she heard a door open, but the suspense ate her alive.

A creak and muffled voices drew her to the door. She had to catch Jack before he went to the parlor and found only the men there.

She took a breath, then cracked her door. She spied her stepmother's back as she strode toward the top of the stairway. Jack stood in his open doorway.

She pulled the door a bit further and hissed to get his attention.

His brows raised, and his head swiveled in her direction. She motioned for him to come into her room.

He dashed over, and she pulled him in, closing the door as quietly as possible. "I don't want my stepmother to hear," she explained.

He swallowed, glancing around the room. "So, this is your room."

She smiled. "Yes, Jack."

"But you said you'd be waiting for me in the parlor."

She nodded. "My father and brother came home. I couldn't wait for you there. We'd have had no privacy to talk."

His tongue slid over his upper lip. "I don't think me being caught in your room is such a good idea."

"We won't get caught," she assured him. "Have a seat." She motioned him to a chair by the window and plopped on her bed.

His gaze swept over her. She liked the way he looked at her. When Randolph's gaze followed her, she had the urge to scrub herself clean, but Jack's gaze made her want to lie back and allow him to have his way with her.

"I can't stay here long, Amanda." His gaze shifted to the door.

"Are you afraid of my father?"

"No, I'm afraid of myself. If we stay in this room much longer…there's no telling what I might do."

Desire glowed in his half-closed eyes. Amanda reveled in the feeling of pure abandon, but they couldn't indulge, not here.

She slid forward on the bed, her elbows on her thighs. "I'll tell you what. You can take me on a picnic."

"A picnic?" Jack frowned.

"Yes. I'll have Mrs. O'Leary pack us a basket, and we'll have our dinner by the pond. We can speak privately there."

Jack wove his fingers together. "The pond? Sounds like an adventure."

She laughed. "Yes. I'll speak to Mrs. O'Leary and when the basket's ready, I'll let you know."

****

Jack paced his room waiting for Amanda's knock. This was a big mistake, especially after promising Erin he'd discourage her stepdaughter. But Amanda hardly gave him a chance to protest. He thought of going downstairs to wait, but knowing her father was home, he didn't feel much like making polite conversation. He'd already feared the man would throw him out if he showed the slightest interest in his daughter. But he did know Jack was a time traveler with no place to go. And although the man seemed a bit stern regarding Amanda, he didn't appear to be heartless. Erin had assured him he wasn't, in any case.

When the soft knock came, Jack was ready. He grabbed his jacket. Amanda had told him men—even those in the working class—didn't go outside the house without their coats and hats.

He opened the door. She stood outside, her cheeks pink. She seemed out of breath.

He grasped her arm. "You okay?"

She smiled. "Of course. I was just getting everything prepared. The others are sitting down at the table, but our basket is all packed."

"Your cook sounds like Wonder Woman!" Jack exclaimed.

Amanda quirked a brow. "Well, yes, she is a

wonder. It's the reason Father hired her."

He laughed and took her hand. "I can see I have a lot to teach you." His thumb brushed her palm.

She let out a tiny gasp and lowered her lashes. When she returned his gaze, he read desire in those blue eyes. A picnic, away from the rest of her family, might just be the ideal place for them to talk…or do other things.

****

Jack unfolded the tablecloth Amanda handed him and spread it over the blanket she'd brought for them to sit on. A slight breeze off the pond might have made the day chilly, but brilliant sunshine in a clear blue sky warmed the day enough to make being outside pleasant.

"Jack, look." Amanda pointed to the other side of the pond where a small group of children frolicked with a mother duck and her chicks. As the birds gobbled up the crusts they threw out to them, the boys and a girl laughed and giggled.

Jack grinned. "Looks like they're having fun."

Amanda gathered her skirts and settled on the edge of the blanket, then beckoned for Jack to join her.

He sat then leaned toward the basket. "Just what did the multi-talented Mrs. O'Leary send us?" He lifted the lid off the basket and inhaled. "Mmmm. Chicken and it's still warm."

Amanda laughed. "You say the strangest things, Jack." She lifted two plates and set them out, but Jack couldn't wait. He grabbed a chicken leg and bit into it.

Amanda pursed her lips, but soon a smile lit up her face. "You are so outrageous, sir."

"What?" Jack took another bite. "I'm hungry and the smell of this food is driving me nuts!"

Amanda shook her head. She lifted out a piece of chicken and set it on her plate, then riffled through the basket. "We have red potatoes, too, and green beans."

"Thumbs up on the potatoes, but I can do without the beans, if you don't mind."

"As you wish." Amanda doled out potatoes on both plates and a dollop of beans on her own, then handed Jack a fork.

He stabbed a potato and raised it to his lips. Before biting into it, he noted Amanda's quirked brow.

"What is it now?"

She waved a hand. "Nothing at all. Go ahead and eat."

He bit into the potato relishing the flavor. He wouldn't mind staying in this century so much with a great cook like Mrs. O'Leary feeding him.

As he devoured the chicken and potatoes, he noticed Amanda picked at the food on her plate.

"Not hungry?" he asked.

She gazed at him, licking her lips. "It's just…I can't stop thinking of how you kissed me." Her face colored, and she glanced toward the pond.

"Oh." Jack swallowed, suddenly ashamed. He was doing the exact opposite of what he'd promised Erin. "Was it good?" he asked feeling lame.

She dropped her gaze, but smiled. "Oh, yes. It was very good." She glanced up. "The best I've ever felt with a man."

"How many men…" Jack stopped himself.

She shrugged. "I haven't been with any man, except for a quick peck on the cheek. It isn't proper for an unmarried woman, you know." Her gaze bore into his.

"Of course." His face heated. "It was a stupid question. I mean…I forgot about how things are in this time period."

She bit her lip. "So, it's different in your time, I gather."

Jack gulped. He really hadn't planned to get into a discussion of future dating customs. He was sure they didn't even call it dating here. Courting maybe?

"Amanda…" He leaned close, so close her sweet breath tickled his cheek. "I'd like to kiss you again, if it's okay."

She glanced around, then nodded.

He scooted closer, to enfold his arms around her back and draw her close. Leaning toward her mouth, he noted her eyes closing as her lips parted on a sigh.

He lowered his mouth and kissed her, lightly swirling the tip of his tongue into her mouth. She didn't resist, her body pliant in his arms. She pressed herself closer as he angled her so she partially lay beneath him. He deepened the kiss causing his body to react, his erection pressing against her belly.

He longed to lie beside her, but the fact they were outside in a public location, reined him in. He released her.

Her eyes fluttered open wide. "Oh, Jack," she gasped. "That was so—so wonderful."

"Glad you liked it." Jack grinned. He glanced around. "I hope no one here took note of us."

Amanda pursed her lips. "I can guarantee we'll be the talk of the town come tomorrow." She brushed out her skirt.

"You think?" Jack frowned as he pondered the implications of what he'd just done. Her father wouldn't much like him taking liberties with his daughter. And if Erin found out, she'd be furious.

Amanda patted his arm. "Don't worry so, Jack."

"But I do." He gazed out over the pond. "I don't belong here and sure haven't a clue how to act."

"You're doing fine," she assured him.

"But if your father finds out about this…" Jack frowned.

"Don't worry about Father. I'll straighten out any misunderstandings with him." She leaned toward Jack. "Besides, if I'm going with you to the future, I have to learn how women act there."

Jack's pulse raced. How could he tell her?

"Amanda, I…" He stopped unable to voice what he needed to say.

She leaned close, brushing a finger over his lip, sending a wave of desire to take her and make her his own in every way.

"Jack, what is it…what's wrong?" She frowned.

"I can't take you with me…" His gaze bore into hers. "…to the future."

Her gaze dropped. "But it might be possible."

"No, Erin says it's not possible." He swallowed. "Besides, a woman like you would never fit into my life."

Amanda's gaze grew cold. She stood, grasping the empty basket, and stalked off.

Chapter Twelve

Jack raced after Amanda, but she sprinted ahead, evading his grasp. How could he take advantage of her when he'd never intended to take her with him?

She stumbled in the front door, dropping the empty basket in the foyer. Racing up the stairs to her room, she slammed the door and collapsed on her bed.

Jack was a rake and a liar. Why had she allowed him to kiss her?

Later in the day, Erin knocked at the door, begging to speak with her, but she wasn't ready to talk to anyone. She needed time to wallow and mourn for the loss of something wonderful now grown ugly.

The following day at the newspaper office, Amanda tried to concentrate on making up questions for an upcoming interview of a local farmer's wife who'd raised a record-breaking hog.

She leaned her elbow on the table and cupped her forehead in her hand. If only her family still lived in Philadelphia. Her father had moved them to this small town after finding a position in a local bank and thought it a good place to raise children, better than in a big city.

But Amanda dreamed of working for a big city paper, a prestigious paper, unlike the small town rag with a pompous editor who thought himself the ideal match for her.

She doodled on a notepad while her thoughts drifted to Jack and his future life. What must it be like to live in such a magical place? He'd certainly want to go back, unlike her stepmother, since he didn't really care for Amanda. Erin had obviously stayed to be with Amanda's father. What other appeal would this backward century have for her? It would be like Amanda finding herself amid pilgrims at Plymouth Rock.

"Amanda." A male voice drew her from her reverie.

She glanced up to find Randolph standing at the open door. His fierce scowl told her he wasn't here for pleasantries.

She straightened in her chair, awaiting his approach.

He stepped into the room and placed both hands on the tabletop across from her. "I've heard talk in town that I don't like."

Amanda frowned. "Talk about what?"

"Your shameful behavior at the pond yesterday." He leaned forward, looming above her.

She swallowed. "Yesterday?" Her pulse raced as she tried to come up with an explanation.

"You and your houseguest, as if you didn't know." He stepped around the table to hover at her back. When he leaned forward, his breath, smelling of onions and something sour caused her to turn her head toward the window.

"Yes, I took Jack out for a picnic. He's feeling better now and needed to get some fresh air."

Randolph's tapered finger lifted her chin, forcing her to look up at him. "I was told…" His voice lowered.

"...the two of you were kissing and engaging in otherwise scandalous embraces."

Amanda gulped. "We've gotten to know one another quite well while he's been recuperating at my home. We were only showing what we feel for each other." She gazed at Randolph boldly.

He took a step back and glanced out the window. "I thought you had feelings for me, but you never expressed it like that."

"Randolph, I...I never felt that strongly about you. You must understand—"

"I expressed my desire to court you, but I wanted to go through proper channels like a gentleman, not a drooling animal."

"Jack is not a..." Amanda swiveled in her chair to face Randolph. "I can't force my feelings. My stepmother raised me to be true to what I want in life, not to submit to a man's whims."

"Your stepmother." Randolph nodded. "She's an eccentric one, isn't she? Probably a member of one of those groups of hysterical women, who think they can behave as men."

Amanda bristled. "My stepmother is a writer, who believes everyone is entitled to live the way they want."

"Your father should chain her in the cellar for teaching you to behave so outrageously. Did she encourage you to pursue this 'Jack'? Where did he come from anyway?"

"He's none of your concern." Amanda swiveled back and propped her hands on the table interlacing her fingers. She had a hard time believing she defended Jack after he'd hurt her. But she wanted to discourage Randolph's attention.

Randolph stepped around the table to face her. "If you won't tell me, I'll speak to your father. Surely, he won't be happy when he learns of your behavior in public."

Amanda's face heated. "You wouldn't dare."

Randolph's brows lifted. "Wouldn't I? I think your father would take offense at a man staying in his own house who would take such liberties with his daughter. Besides, you said Mr. Lawton had recovered enough to accompany you on a picnic. Surely, he can return to his home, wherever that may be."

Amanda longed to wipe the smug smile from the editor's face. "He doesn't remember where he lives."

"Extraordinary." Randolph sneered. "Perhaps you should write an article for the paper. Ask anyone if they know who the man is and where he lives."

Amanda straightened, lifting her chin. "My parents and I are working on finding his home. But we can't exactly throw the poor man out into the streets. It wouldn't be Christian."

"Nevertheless, I plan to have a word with your father at my first opportunity."

Amanda shrugged, feigning indifference. "Do what you wish, Randolph. I have to get back to work now."

Randolph huffed. She glanced up to find him glaring but lowered her head to her notepad. She'd not allow his threats to intimidate her.

She didn't look up again until his footsteps retreated. Standing, she stepped to the window and bit her lip. She wondered what her father would have to say when Randolph told him about the picnic.

****

Jack paced the small confines of the parlor, his

hands clenched. He glanced at Amanda wringing her hands by the open window.

"He can't threaten you like this, Amanda. I don't care if he's your boss. You can find another job."

"Not so easy, Jack. This town is so small it only has one paper. I couldn't find another job as a reporter unless I moved away." She crossed her arms over her chest. "And what do you care anyway?"

Jack gulped and lowered his gaze. "I don't really have a choice in the matter. I belong in my time as you belong in yours."

Amanda stepped in front of him, halting his pacing. "You must see what a tenuous position I'm in. And if I have to stay here without you, maybe I shouldn't discourage Randolph."

Jack's face heated. "You're not telling me you've kissed him?"

"Jack…" Amanda sighed. "I allowed him to take me out to dinner on a few occasions, but no, I've never let him get near enough to kiss me."

Jack smiled. "But you let me."

Her face colored. "I shouldn't have."

Jack chose to ignore her statement, clasped his hands behind his back and continued pacing. "So, Randolph plans to tell your father someone saw us kissing?"

"And embracing…scandalously," Amanda amended.

Jack snickered. "If he could see how people live in my century. What we did wouldn't even have been noticed."

Amanda's lips thinned into a firm line. "Please don't speak of it."

Jack frowned. "For now, what do we do about your father if Randolph tells him about us? Will he be pi—I mean, angry?"

"I don't know." Amanda shook her head. "Although he's a bit more modern thinking than most girl's fathers, he's still rather protective of me."

"Would he throw me out?"

"Erin wouldn't let him."

Jack shoved both hands into his pockets. "Good to know someone's on my side."

Amanda stepped closer. "I'm on your side, Jack. Don't forget that. You're the one who doesn't want me."

Jack shrugged. "I'm sorry, Amanda."

She tapped a finger against her lip. "What if you can't get back?" She lowered her gaze. "You could always stay here. Erin's managed to live here all these years."

Jack scratched his head. "I don't know. I do have a life back there, after all."

Amanda turned away. "Of course, you're dead set on getting home." She glanced back. "You're not married, are you?"

"No."

"You don't have a sweetheart?"

"No, Amanda. I'm a single guy who lives alone. No attachments."

"Then why are you so hard pressed to go back there? It sounds like a lonely way to live."

Jack sighed. "Knowing someone like you wants to be with me will make it all that much harder to go back."

Amanda smiled and grasped his hand. "You really

do care! If you can't take me with you, stay. You have a skill you can use here to make a living. Why not stay?"

Jack lifted her hand and kissed the back of it. "I think we should deal with things as they come. We have to do something about Randolph. If he tells your father…"

She bit her lip. "I'll deal with Father and Randolph."

Jack's face heated. "I swear to God, Amanda, if Randolph as much as looks at you funny, I'll kill him."

"Shhh, Jack. I've worked for him for nearly two months. I can handle him. I have to go now, but I'll see you tonight." She left the room.

Jack turned to the window. She stepped from the house and strode down the street, her felt hat bobbing. He meant what he said about Randolph. If the man so much as touched Amanda, he'd regret it.

Chapter Thirteen

Will Montgomery paced the small confines of the parlor. The scent of cigar smoke hung in the air. Amanda twisted her hands in the folds of her skirt as she waited for her father to speak.

Her stepmother had caught her when she arrived home from the newspaper indicating her father wanted to see both of them in the parlor before supper.

Erin stepped to the window and raised it allowing the smoke to dissipate. Her father paced for a few minutes, his expression unreadable. Amanda swallowed, wishing he would just get what he had to say out in the open.

He gestured to the settee. "If you ladies would please sit."

Amanda gathered her skirts and perched on the seat beside Erin.

"What is it, Father?"

He didn't take a seat but stood glowering at both of them.

"It appears our houseguest is sufficiently recovered. Mr. Lawton needs to leave our home and find a place of his own."

"But, Will…" Erin half rose from her seat. "You know his circumstances. We can't just throw him out. He has no other place to go."

Will raised a hand. "I understand your concerns,

darlin'. But his staying on any longer, now that he's healed, will surely compromise Amanda's reputation."

"Father!" Amanda protested.

Her father's glare silenced her.

"I've been made aware of you and Mr. Lawton putting on a public display at the pond the other day."

"But, you don't understand—"

"I think the close proximity of Mr. Lawton in this house and his fanciful stories of the future have enticed you, Amanda. I'd hate to see this escalate into an improper situation."

Amanda glanced at Erin. Her stepmother's mouth set in a thin, straight line.

"What kind of situation are you referring to?" Amanda asked.

"A situation where he goes back to his time and leaves you compromised, or worse yet, with child."

"Father!" Amanda's face flamed.

Erin clasped her hands in her lap but said nothing.

"I want him out of this house within the next two days," Will said.

"But, Will…" Erin stood.

Amanda did, too. "If he goes, I go."

"Amanda!" Erin grasped Amanda's arm. "We'll work this out."

"Mother," Amanda protested. "He's listening to lies Randolph told him."

"What are you saying?" Erin glanced from Amanda to Will.

"Randolph has been after me to marry him. He wants Jack out of the picture. He threatened to tell Father about me and Jack by the pond. But he didn't see us. He's just going on hearsay."

Her father bit the tip off a new cigar. "Are you telling me Randolph is lying?"

"Well…" Amanda shrugged. "I did take Jack on a picnic. Thought he needed to get out of the house and get some fresh air."

"But he told me you two…" His face colored.

"Mother." Amanda glanced at Erin. "Tell him it's nothing."

"I…ah…" Erin flushed. "I think it was likely very innocent, Will. Randolph is obviously jealous."

"Nevertheless," Will said, "I'll not have folks gossiping about my daughter. Jack won't be staying."

Erin bit her lip. "Why don't we get him a room at the hotel?" She nodded at Amanda and set her gaze on her husband. "Just until we see if a way can be found to send him home."

Will scowled, but slowly nodded. "I suppose that'll do. For now."

After her father left the room, Amanda grasped her stepmother's hand. "Thank you. At least I'll know Jack isn't alone on the street."

"It's the least I could do. After all, I was once in the same situation. He'll be glad to have a place to stay until we can figure a way to get him home."

****

Amanda and Erin escorted Jack to the hotel. As he'd packed, Amanda had assured him it was a decent place and being just across town, easily accessible for both her and Erin to pay him visits.

Erin checked him in and insisted on seeing him to the room. Amanda tagged along, thinking this her chance to see exactly where Jack would be staying.

The bed looked and felt comfy. The room had a

washstand and a mirror with a dresser plenty big enough for Jack's one change of clothes.

"This'll do fine, Erin." Jack smiled, but Amanda read tension in his stance. He surely must be terrified of being left alone in this place.

Erin performed a perfunctory check of the room and, once satisfied, drew Amanda aside. "We'd best go and let Jack get settled for the night. We'll be back tomorrow to go over plans to find a way for you to get home."

"Thank you." Jack nodded. "Both of you. I don't know what would've become of me if Amanda hadn't found me and brought me to your home."

Amanda's eyes misted. She didn't want to leave him here alone, but maybe it was for the best. If he really didn't want her…

Erin caught her gaze. "Come, Amanda."

She drew in a sharp breath. "Mother, if I could have just a moment alone with Jack?"

Erin bit her lip, but nodded. "I'll wait in the hall, but be quick."

Once her stepmother stepped from the room and the door clicked shut, Amanda approached Jack, longing to race into his arms and beg him not to leave.

"I suppose this is goodbye, Jack," she said.

He gathered her so close, her breasts crushed against his hard chest. Her head told her to pull away and leave, but the vibration of his heartbeat stayed her.

"It'll be all right." His lips brushed her cheek.

She tilted her traitorous lips toward his and found his mouth. She eagerly opened tasting his manly scent.

When he released her, he grinned. "Your step-mom is waiting outside. You'd better get going. We'll see each other tomorrow."

She shook her head. "I don't know if we should see each other again."

He frowned. "Amanda, I don't want to leave things like this."

"If you can't take me with you, we've no other choice."

She backed toward the door, then slipped out. Her last sight of Jack, his hands shoved into his pockets, his eyes downcast. She joined Erin for the walk back to the house, vowing to forget she'd ever met him.

****

Jack dozed fitfully in the strange bed. He'd grown accustomed over the past week to sleeping in the Montgomery home, but it took days before he felt as if he wasn't living in a dream and would soon wake.

But as he recovered, knowing Amanda slept just down the hall was a temptation he couldn't entertain. This century was so repressed, and he'd never do anything to hurt Amanda, even if it meant denying his feelings for her.

He recalled the photo he'd carried to the house the night of the accident. What had happened to it? And what had happened to him?

Erin's theory that they both inhabited bodies they'd had in a past life, seemed plausible. More so than the idea he'd traveled inter-dimensionally to get here. But considering either possibility seemed crazy.

He had no other way to explain it, though, and hoped he still had a live body in his own time to go back to. He tossed and finally rose to step from the braided rug beside his bed onto the cool wood floor.

He tried to adjust his eyes to the hint of a glow

from the half moon. He fumbled on the nightstand and lit the oil lamp. Amanda had told him some of the big cities, like nearby Philadelphia, now had electricity, but it hadn't come to this small town yet.

Stepping to the washstand, he splashed tepid water on his face. Indoor plumbing was another innovation relegated to the big cities, but not everyone had it.

He fumbled for the pocket watch Erin had given him so he could keep track of time. *Two-thirty in the morning.* He may as well climb back into bed and try to get a few more hours of sleep. What else could he do?

At home, he'd reach for the remote and try to find an old movie to lull him. He didn't even have a book to read but guessed that's what people did in this century when sleep refused to come.

He sighed and stepped toward the bed, prepared to give sleep another try. Before he could pull the sheet back, a scraping at the door sent a chill up his spine. Was someone trying to break in?

Creeping toward the door, he tried to rationalize what someone would be doing in the hall at this hour. Could it be a hotel worker?

He pressed his ear against the wood and held his breath. The scraping stopped. Jack cracked the door, prepared to slam it shut if a knife wielding intruder stood outside ready to rob him.

"Jack." The whisper of a female voice sounded familiar.

"Amanda?" Her flowery, womanly scent drifted to him.

"Let me in," she hissed, "before someone sees me."

He yanked her inside and shut the door. Her breath rasped as if she'd been running. He stepped to the night table and lit the gas lamp.

"What the hell are you doing here?" he demanded.

Her brow furrowed. "I came to see you. I couldn't sleep thinking you'd go back and I'd never see you again."

"But you can't just come here in the middle of the night."

Her full lips puckered. "You really don't want me."

"Amanda." He sighed. "It's dangerous for a woman to be wandering the streets alone in the middle of the night. In this century or mine." He grasped her shoulders. "What were you thinking?"

"I was thinking of how much I want to be with you..." She hesitated. "In this room." Her lowered voice grew sultry. "Just the two of us."

"You mean...?" Jack sputtered. "You want to..."

She settled on the bed leaning back languorously. "I want to be with you in every way a man and woman can." Her cheeks colored, but her gaze held his. "Please, Jack."

Jack swallowed as his body heated. "But you've never..." His words trailed off.

She shook her head. "No. I've never been with a man." She reached a hand toward him. "If I have to live without you, at least show me what I'll miss. Teach me."

He gulped. "Are you absolutely sure?"

She patted the mattress. "Yes. I want you to show me how it feels to be a woman."

He settled beside her. "But I haven't got any protection. And you're a...a..."

"A virgin," she finished for him. A frown creased her brow. "Protection?"

He waved a hand. "You know. From pregnancy."

"Oh!" She bit her lip. "I don't really know much about these things. But Erin would."

"Your mother?" Jack shook his head. "I don't think consulting her would be a good idea."

"But Jack…" Her hand slid up his bared arm, then across his chest, a slim finger twirling through the hair close to his nipple. His groin tightened as waves of desire sent his shaft pushing against the fabric of his drawers.

"Amanda." He sighed. "I think you should go now. This isn't the right time."

Her hand slid lower, teasing the band of his drawers.

He bit back an oath. "If you don't leave now, I can't be responsible for my actions."

She ran her tongue over her lower lip. "Jack, we may never have this chance again. I need to be with you…oh, my!"

Her hand slid down the length of his erection, sending sparks throughout his body. If he didn't stop her, it would all be over in a few minutes. He grasped her hand and gently moved it onto her lap.

"You really don't know much about men, do you?"

Her gaze focused on the bulge in his drawers. "Of course I know about a man's anatomy." Her face reddened. "But I hadn't realized…"

He grinned, unable to resist teasing her, despite his discomfort. "I really do need to protect you. The last thing I want is to leave you pregnant."

"Wouldn't matter if you were taking me with you."

He shook his head. "I don't think it's possible for you to go forward in time. I'm not even sure I can get back."

She drew in a long shuddering breath. "I don't care. I want to be with you. I don't care about the consequences."

"You say that now…"

"I mean it, Jack. If I can't spend my life with you, I'd be more than happy to bear and raise your child."

He sighed. "Maybe we can figure a way to lower the risk. When did you last have a period?"

She frowned.

"I mean…what do you call it in this century?" He pointed to her belly. "When did you last bleed?"

"Oh! You mean my flow." She chewed on her lip. "I finished a few days ago."

"Okay. That's good. Means it's probably safe. But I can pull out to make it safer."

She frowned again, but nodded. "Whatever you think is best."

"And you're absolutely sure you want to do this?"

She gazed toward the window. "Yes, and we'd better hurry it along, before daybreak comes. I've got to get back to my room without being seen."

"Talk about pressure." Jack leaned back lying flat on the bed.

Amanda perched over him. "Please don't say no. I couldn't bear it."

Her eyes glowed in the lantern light. Her scent and touch sent waves of desire flowing into him. This wouldn't take long on his part, but he worried about it being her first time. He didn't want to rush it.

Her hand slid down his chest to his shaft. He reached up and cupped her cheek as she lowered her face to his. Their lips found each other and the thrill of having her in his bed, in his life, sent his pulse racing.

He fingered the top clasp of her dress, fumbling to open it and expose her throat. She sat up and unhooked the front of the dress down to her waist.

He sat and pushed the top half of the dress off her shoulders, noting the skirt was still fastened. He grinned. "Not used to these nineteenth century dresses."

She smiled. "Then I'll have to help you." She stood and unhooked the skirt, allowing the garment to float to her feet.

His gaze drifted over her. She wore a frilly, white sleeveless garment covering her chest and—from the waist down—full white skirts that reached to an inch above the floor. "You're still wearing an awful lot of clothes."

She tilted her head. "Jack, these are my under garments."

"That's your underwear?" He whistled. "Women in my day wear a lot less than that when fully clothed."

Her face turned pink. "How scandalous, Jack!" She clapped her hands. "Talking about where you come from makes me sad, though, realizing I'll never share it with you."

"I wish I could take you there." He reached a hand toward her. "But for now…"

She untied a string at her waist and the under skirts slid down to join the patterned skirt on the floor. She stepped out of the heap of material and settled beside him on the bed.

"You call this undressed?" he muttered. White pants covered her thighs and knees and the sleeveless garment covered the upper half of her body.

Easing her onto her back, he poised above her.

"Let's see how much more we can uncover."

She trembled beneath him, but her gaze held his.

****

Amanda thrilled to Jack's touch as he slid his hand over the exposed skin at her throat, scandalously close to the crease between her breasts. She drew in a gasp of delight.

"Am I hurting you?" Jack's concerned frown drew a giggle from Amanda.

"No, it feels wonderful."

He nodded and slid his hand lower, beneath the top of her camisole.

Tingles shot over her body, intensifying with every inch of skin he touched. She shifted on the bed, allowing him to draw up the garment and expose her breasts. She shivered.

His heated gaze drifted over her, his lips tilting upward. "You are making yourself very hard to resist."

She grinned. "I don't want you to leave me, Jack."

He kissed first one breast, then the other, catching a nipple between his teeth.

His suckling sent intense waves of pleasure spiraling to Amanda's belly, and her woman parts. "Oh, Jack!" she gasped.

She grasped the button at the waist of her drawers and opened them, exposing her bared belly to his attentions. His lips lingered on her belly button, then traveled down.

Amanda closed her eyes and swung her head from side to side wanting to lose herself in the intensity of it all. When his fingers reached her core, she jolted beneath his touch. Hot wetness seeped from the junction between her thighs.

She opened her eyes and caught his smoldering gaze.

"You want more?" he asked.

She gulped. "Yes. Please don't stop."

He rose to his knees, unfastening his drawers, then stood beside the bed and allowed them to drop.

Amanda stared at his muscular thighs, with coarse, dark hair at his center…and oh, my! His shaft stood out straight jiggling to and fro. She reached out a hand, tentatively at first, then slid her finger along its smooth length.

"I take it you've never seen one up close." Jack grinned.

Amanda huffed. "Of course I have, but not this— this…"

He tilted his head as her face heated.

"I didn't realize they grew so—so…"

"It means I'm ready for you, sweetheart. If you are."

Her body ached for his touch. If this would relieve her suffering…"Yes, Jack. Tell me what to do."

"Just lie back. I'll take it real slow."

Amanda eased back, her pulse racing, as Jack guided her into position with her legs apart. He climbed over her supine body, but kept his weight on his elbows. The touch of his shaft at her juncture sent a jolt through her entire body.

"This may hurt, since it's your first time. I'll go slow, but if you want to stop, you tell me."

Amanda nodded, but doubted her throat would work to voice any protest.

"Just relax," Jack coaxed.

Intense tingles washed over her at his touch. He

eased her legs farther apart. She breathed deeply. A pulsing thickness pressed into her and she had the urge to shout at him to stop, but at the same time longed for him to continue.

Cramping pain caused her to bite her lip, but he'd warned her this would happen. *Relax.*

He pulled out, then slowly eased back in. The spiral built again just as when he'd used his fingers. Wave after wave of pleasure built until her senses focused only on him. Small moans escaped her lips, growing into louder ones. She'd never felt anything like this before. Nothing mattered, but this moment with Jack.

She rode the wave, higher and higher, until she shattered into pieces, breathing heavily. Jack collapsed and rolled to her side. His hand covered her cheek. "You okay?"

She licked her lips and nodded. "That was...wonderful, Jack. Is it like this every time?"

He leaned on an elbow and slid a finger along her lower lip. "I hope it will be better next time." He glanced at her belly. "Sorry for the mess. I'd better get you a rag to clean it up."

She glanced down and dipped a finger into the sticky liquid coating her belly.

"Don't move." He rose and padded to the washstand, returning with a wet rag. "I pulled out to prevent pregnancy." He wiped the rag across her, then pressed a dry towel on the spot.

She sighed and settled into the down pillow. Contentment crept over her. She longed to stay here with Jack but had to get back home.

****

After they'd dressed, Jack escorted Amanda to her parents' house but left her at the door. He planted a chaste kiss on her swollen lips before she crept inside.

Back in his hotel room, he paced until dawn lit the sky. *What the hell are you doing, Jack?* If he was able to return to his time what would become of her?

And what if he'd left her pregnant, despite his precautions?

If her stepmother found out, or worse yet, her father, he'd be in it deep. They'd probably demand he stay and marry their daughter. And even if she wasn't pregnant and he returned without her, how could he live with the memory of what he'd lost?

He ran a hand through his tousled hair. Despite what he'd told Erin, he'd find a way to take Amanda with him. He had no choice now. He was head over heels in love with a long-dead woman.

Chapter Fourteen

The following day, Amanda sat at the long table in the outer office of the paper, doodling on her pad. She couldn't concentrate on the story she worked on. The image of Jack's naked body and what they'd done in his room threatened to send her into a swoon. She longed to run over to his hotel room.

Miss Carson sauntered into the room carrying a stack of paper. Her scandalously rouged lips formed into a pout, dark eyes narrowed as she gazed at Amanda.

"Is there a problem, Miss Carson?" Amanda asked.

"Mr. Norwood's told me about that rake, Mr. Lawton, who was staying with your family for a bit."

"What?" Amanda spun in her chair to face the curvy secretary. "What is Randolph saying about him?"

The woman leaned forward, her lips near Amanda's ear. Her cloying scent caused a tickle in Amanda's nose. She fought back the urge to sneeze.

"Mr. Norwood says Mr. Lawton is not who he claims to be." She nodded as if revealing a tantalizing secret.

Amanda bristled. "Why would he say such a thing?" A trace of fear sent shivers down her back. What could he have uncovered about Jack's background?

The secretary shrugged. "He didn't say but must

know something about the man."

Amanda scowled. "Is Mr. Norwood in his office?"

Miss Carson lifted a hand to her throat. "Why, yes?"

Amanda stood, her face heating. "Then I'll just see exactly what he knows." She strode to the door, the secretary on her heels.

"Miss Montgomery, I don't think he'd appreciate you barging in…"

Before the woman could finish the sentence, Amanda pushed open Randolph's door.

Miss Carson gasped. "I'm sorry, Mr. Norwood. She insisted on seeing you." She backed away. Amanda faced Randolph.

He peered over his spectacles and frowned. "Is there a problem, Amanda?"

She strode into the office and stood over his desk. Propping her hands on her hips, she drew in a breath. "What do you know about Mr. Lawton that you're spreading all over town?"

"Ah…" Randolph motioned for her to take a seat.

She gathered her skirts and perched on the edge of the chair closest to the desk.

He propped his elbows on the desk top and laced his fingers. "So you want to know what I've learned about your friend, Mr. Jack Lawton."

Amanda swallowed. "Yes. If the whole town already knows, you'd best tell me."

He leaned back and sneered. "Besides the fact that you and he were behaving outrageously by the pond?"

"Randolph," she hissed. "If you know something about Jack, tell me, so I can set you straight."

"Oh, Jack, is it?" He scowled. "I've done a bit of

research on Mr. Lawton. Seems he's a common workman who lives across town."

Amanda straightened in her chair, her heart thumping. "Across town?" She gulped. "Does he have a family?"

"Seems he had a wife, but she died six months ago of scarlet fever."

"No children?" Amanda asked, hoping to hear in the negative.

"None that I know of."

She settled back in the chair, not allowing Randolph to see the relief she felt at hearing this news.

"But he lives in a hovel with two unruly brothers and their wives. I believe his parents have passed on as well."

Knowing where Jack really came from and that he had no wife or girl waiting for him in this time, added to Amanda's sense of well-being. Nothing Randolph told her now would make a bit of difference.

Randolph's steely gaze pierced her. She shrugged. "So, he's poor and a common workman. This is what you're spreading around town?"

"He and his brothers imbibe quite a bit. I doubt your father would want his sort anywhere near you. And he's definitely not marriage material for a lady like you."

"Who says I want to marry him?"

Randolph sputtered. "He lived in your home for a week!"

"He was gravely injured. It was my family's duty to nurse him back to health."

"But the way you cavorted with him at the pond is all over town. No other man would consider you marriage material."

Amanda's skin prickled. "Well then, I won't be looking for gentlemen callers, will I?" She pinned him with her glare.

He leaned toward her. "I won't allow this man to leave you as spoiled goods, Amanda. I still want you as my wife. Marrying me will make you respectable."

Amanda's pulse raced. "I don't want to marry anyone." She stood and strode out the door.

****

Jack paced the cramped parlor waiting for Amanda to return from work. Her father and brother were at the bank, while Erin and Mrs. O'Leary worked in the kitchen.

Jack didn't know how much longer he could stand living like this. He needed to return to his time but didn't want to leave Amanda. He had no life here, and Erin had told him how hard it had been for her to forgo her life in the future to settle with her husband and family. Jack would never fit into this time as she had. He had to go back.

The outer door creaked open. Jack rushed to the open parlor doorway to peer into the foyer.

Amanda's hat bobbed as she removed the pins. When she caught sight of Jack, her lips curved into a smile.

He stepped forward and grasped her arm. "Come in the parlor. I have to talk to you right now."

Her smile faltered, but she followed him into the room. He closed the doors and leaned against them.

She stepped around the settee but didn't sit. "What is it, Jack?"

He clasped his hands together, his palms moist. "I

need to go home. Now."

Amanda stepped to his side. "Has my stepmother found a way?"

He shook his head. "She can't be sure, but she thinks the room you found me in is the key." He glanced away. "And Erin's brooch with your father's hair."

"Her brooch?" Amanda paced toward the window, lifted the lace curtain and peered outside. "The brooch brought her to my father, but how does she think it will send you back?"

Jack shook his head. "I don't know. But since I no longer have the photo of you Erin believes brought me here, she decided the brooch is worth a try."

"Photo…" Amanda mused. "I may have one I can give you, but it may not be the right one."

Jack's pulse quickened. He cupped Amanda's cheek and planted a kiss on her lips.

She pulled back and gazed at him.

"You have a photograph of yourself? A recent one?"

"Yes, a tintype. I'll get it for you." She stepped to a desk in a corner of the tiny room, opened the top drawer. After rifling through it, she produced a book. "It's in here."

Jack peered over her shoulder. She opened a book full of old black-and-white photographs. At least they looked old to him. Each photo was five by eight inside a gilded oval with a decorative border.

She stopped at a page with a photo of her.

He gazed at the picture. "This is it." He pointed to the photo. "The framed photo was hanging in the house, and I had the picture with me when I got hit with the beam."

"This was hanging in Randolph's house?" Amanda's mouth turned down.

Jack fingered the edges of the photo. "Yes. Why would it be hanging in the house?"

She lifted a hand to her mouth. Her fingers trembled. "It must mean I married Randolph. I was his wife." Her wide gaze lifted to catch Jack's.

"Not necessarily." He shook his head. "Maybe he just has a thing for you and found a copy of this photo."

"A thing?" Amanda asked. "What kind of thing?"

Jack chuckled. "I mean, he likes you. You said he wants to marry you."

"I would never…" Amanda plopped onto the settee clasping both hands in her lap. "…but what if I had no other choice."

Jack gazed at her. "Everyone has a choice who they want to marry."

"Maybe in your time, Jack, but not in mine." She rose and clasped his hand. "You can't go unless you take me with you."

"Amanda." Jack sighed. "I'd love to take you, but what if we can't be together?"

Her gaze dropped. "Then I'm doomed, I fear."

"Don't say that."

She reached up to cup his chin, then stood on her toes to offer her lips. The kiss sent shivers down Jack's spine. He couldn't leave her to an uncertain fate. He deepened the kiss, and she responded with a soft moan, tightening her arms around his back.

"I won't leave you, Amanda," he said. "I swear."

Chapter Fifteen

Amanda's feet barely touched ground as she hurried from the mercantile to her home. Jack had promised to take her to the future. A time where women were equal to men and she could marry anyone she liked. Or not marry at all if she chose.

She'd left the house with a light shawl on the sunny and mild April morning, but ended up carrying the wrap over one arm. She couldn't wait to see Jack, who'd promised to stop by today.

After entering the house, she hung her shawl on a peg, pulled the hatpin, and set her felt hat on the shelf. The open window at the far side of the foyer allowed a fresh breeze to circulate through the house.

She stepped toward the kitchen doorway but stopped at the sound of male voices in the parlor behind the closed doors.

Had Jack stopped by early, or could it be her father and brother? She pressed her ear to the door to try to make out what they said.

"I know Mr. Lawton no longer is staying in your home, but as long as he's in town, he's a threat to Amanda's reputation."

She gasped. That sounded like Randolph.

"I understand your concern, sir," her father said, "but she is my daughter, and I trust her to do the right thing."

She pressed a hand to her mouth. At least her father was on her side.

"But sir, it's not just Amanda you have to consider. What do you know of this Mr. Lawton?"

"He seemed like a decent fellow when he stayed with us."

Footsteps told Amanda one of the men had stepped toward the door. She shrank back, afraid they'd discover her eavesdropping.

"I've done research on Jack Lawton." Randolph's voice was close to the door.

Amanda pressed herself against the wall.

"He's from a low-class family on the other side of town. He's a common workman and a hard drinker."

Her father cleared his throat. "I don't think we need to be concerned. He's moving on, so he's told us. He just needed time to recover."

"I fear he may seek out Amanda and try to compromise her even further than he already has." Footsteps moved away from the door as if Randolph stepped toward her father. "If I marry her now, she'd be spared trying to find a man who wouldn't be bothered by a tarnished reputation."

"Mr. Norwood…" her father began.

"Call me Randolph, sir. I hope to be part of your family very soon. I'm building a house a few blocks from here for my future wife and family. Your daughter would be close by, along with any grandchildren that come along."

Amanda held in her outburst, longing to push the door open and put a stop to Randolph's male posturing. How dare he?

"I'm sorry, Randolph," her father said. "Amanda is

her own woman. I'd dare not influence her in the choice of husband. If she chooses to marry, it will be her decision."

"But sir—"

Amanda bit back a grin. Her father really was a modern thinking man.

"If my daughter doesn't choose to marry you, there's not much I can do."

"Then I fear we have nothing more to discuss," Randolph said.

Heavy footsteps approached the door. Amanda scrambled toward the kitchen door and slipped inside. She peered through the crack in the door as Randolph stormed from the parlor and out of the house.

****

Jack dressed and left the hotel. He needed to see Erin about the plans to send him back home. He also had to see Amanda. The longing he held for her since their intimate encounter in his room, left no doubt in his mind that he couldn't go home without her. She was now his life and would leave a huge void if he left her in the past.

As he passed the mercantile, remembering to tip his hat to all the ladies strolling by, he caught sight of Randolph riding in a one-horse carriage. The man's nose tilted up at an arrogant angle. Jack hated to think of Amanda married to the bastard. He'd do whatever he could to prevent it.

Doubling his pace, Jack hurried to the Montgomery house. He strode to the porch but hesitated at the front door. Although he'd lived here for a week, he couldn't just barge in. He rapped and waited for someone to answer.

The door flew open. "Oh, Jack!" Amanda gasped. "I am so glad to see you."

Before he could utter a response, she grabbed his arm and yanked him inside.

Her scent drifted to him as he reached out to cup her cheek.

"Jack," she breathed.

Footsteps from the staircase alerted Jack that they weren't alone. "I came to see your stepmother." He averted his face from Amanda's luscious lips, so close to his.

"Mrs. O'Leary." Amanda turned as the cook ambled toward them. "Is my mother home?"

"In the kitchen she is, I do believe." The older woman beamed. "Why hello, Jack. Good to see you again."

"Hello, ma'am. I'm here to see Mrs. Montgomery."

"I'm heading that way. I'll fetch her." The cook angled her frame through the kitchen doorway.

Amanda turned to Jack. "Is she planning to try to send you home?" Her lips turned downward.

"I'm not sure. I have to talk to her." His lips were inches from hers. "And to you afterward. Don't go anywhere."

Erin stepped from the kitchen, her gaze fixed on the pair. "Come into the parlor, Jack. We have a lot to discuss."

Amanda folded her arms across her chest as her gaze narrowed.

Jack nodded to Erin. "Be right in."

Erin strode to the parlor doors and opened them wide. She hesitated, looked back for a final glance, then stepped inside.

Jack turned to Amanda. He grasped her shoulders and pulled her to him for a quick kiss. "Wait for me. I have to talk to you before I go."

She nodded, but frowned.

After a final glance at Amanda, Jack stepped through the doors and closed them behind him.

Chapter Sixteen

Amanda crept to her parents' room while her stepmother and Jack remained occupied in the parlor. She had to get hold of the brooch and hoped Erin didn't already have it with her. She searched her stepmother's jewelry box but didn't see anything resembling a hair brooch. Discouraged, she turned to leave but on a hunch felt around the bottom of the felt lined box and discovered a false bottom.

Her breath caught as she lifted the edge and exposed the jewelry inside. A brooch! She recognized the dark chocolate-brown hair. Her father's hair had dulled over time with streaks of gray running through it, but this was undoubtedly his hair.

She held the brooch up to the window to inspect it closely. The decorative oval frame held glass covering intricately woven strands of hair. If this brooch had sent Erin back to this time, could it send Jack to the future?

She crept from the room, carefully closing the door so not to alert anyone downstairs, and hurried to her own room. Her photo now sat on her dresser, so she'd have it to give to Jack when he...they, returned to Randolph's house.

Packing both objects into a large drawstring bag, she returned to the foyer so Jack couldn't leave without her seeing him.

She sat by the staircase waiting for him to come to

her.

****

Jack shook his head. "I'm sorry, Erin, but how can you expect me to leave without at least trying to take Amanda along?"

Erin's lips thinned to a straight line. "You promised me you wouldn't. It's likely not possible anyway."

Jack ran a hand through his hair. "I kind of promised her I'd at least try." He locked gazes with Erin.

She propped her hands on her hips. "You shouldn't have, Jack. I can't allow you to take her with you."

"Are you going to the house?"

"I—I suppose I should. I won't go into the house though. Don't want to take the chance of being drawn to the future with you."

He nodded. If she didn't go in, maybe he could find a way to sneak Amanda in without her stepmother's knowledge.

"Jack, please believe me, I'm only thinking of my daughter. If she went with you, she'd be lost to us forever."

Jack sighed. "I guess I understand. But what if you had to leave your husband behind? Could you do it?"

"We're not even talking about the same thing here. You've only known Amanda for what…a couple of weeks?"

"But you said after you'd returned to the future, you willed yourself back here."

"I did. But I'd known Will a lot longer than a few weeks. We'd been through so much."

"I feel as though I've known your daughter a

lifetime and then some," he protested.

Erin shook her head. "After a few weeks in this time, I would've given my eyeteeth to go back. Will wasn't even a consideration at that point. I didn't know him well enough."

Jack shrugged. "I guess you know best."

"I do," she stated. "Now, let me find the brooch so we can send you on your way."

****

Amanda glanced up as the parlor door opened. She caught Jack's guarded gaze and her stepmother's resigned one. "I'll be right back, Jack."

Erin ascended the stairs.

After she was out of earshot, Amanda pulled Jack toward the parlor doorway. "Where's she going?"

"To get the brooch."

Amanda's face heated. "Oh, no. We've got to get out of here right now!"

"Why?" Jack's brows drew together.

"She won't find the brooch, because I've got it."

"You do? Where?"

She lifted the bag. "Right here, along with the photograph. We've got to hurry before she comes back." She grasped his sleeve and led him to the door.

"Where are we going? We can't go to the house in broad daylight."

"I know a place we can hide out until dark. Trust me, Jack."

She led him around the back of the house. Erin would think they'd gone to the kitchen, and by the time she realized they'd left the house, they'd be out of sight. Amanda hoped Jack would follow her lead. In the short time she'd known him, she'd fallen hopelessly in love and couldn't allow him to disappear from her life. She longed for the chance to explore the world of the future with him.

Jack followed Amanda's lead to Randolph's house. They hung back and observed workmen stepping in and out. "Where can we go?" Jack whispered.

"Come with me." Amanda grasped his hand and led him to the back of the house. A grove of trees stood several yards behind the structure.

Amanda pointed. "We'll hide in there and watch. They'll likely leave at dusk."

Jack nodded and crept into the grove after her. He glanced at the house, hoping the workers didn't spot them. Once in the chilled shade of the trees, he looked back again. The house was still visible between fragrant flowering branches and shrubs amid a few evergreens. They wouldn't be seen as long as they stayed hidden.

She settled on a pile of dried leaves spreading her skirts under her like a blanket. "Come sit with me," she said.

He sat cross-legged beside her. "So, what do we do? Just hang out here until dusk?"

"Hang out?"

He shrugged. "Another of my modern expressions. I meant, do we just sit here?"

She giggled. "I can think of things we can do to occupy our time." She drew him close and nuzzled his cheek, then brushed her lips over his.

Her scent and taste sent his heart racing. If these were to be the last moments he spent with her, he'd make the best of it.

Gathering her softness to him, he kissed her thoroughly. He didn't want to go any further for fear of being discovered, but his body reacted otherwise. He cupped her breast, but her corset got in the way.

"This thing is worse than a bra," he muttered.

"A what?" She gazed at him, her eyebrows lifting.

"An undergarment women wear in my time to keep their breasts harnessed."

"Harnessed?" She laughed.

"Amanda, I don't know if we should go any further."

She lifted her skirts to reveal her ankles and calves. "Please, Jack, I'm so afraid of losing you."

"But I can't take the chance."

"I told you I'll accept any babe you leave me with. At least I'll have a part of you with me if you go."

He shook his head. "No. I don't think…" He bit his lip, then smiled. "Wait, there is a way."

She frowned. He climbed over her, capturing her lips. "I can pleasure you without taking the chance of leaving you pregnant. I should have thought of this before."

He pushed her petticoats away and lowered his face between her legs. Parting the white cotton drawers, he exposed her white skin. He stroked her inner thigh until she shivered.

"Oh, Jack." Her breathy voice quivered. "What are you doing down there?"

"You'll see." He blew lightly on her inner folds until she gasped. "Jack, I've never felt anything like that before."

"There's more." Inserting a finger into her, he twirled the soft, wet folds. She was definitely up to the task.

Her fingers worked into his hair. "Jack, I don't

think you should…"

"Don't worry. You'll like this."

She lay back, breathing heavily.

****

Amanda had never felt such a wondrous thing in her life. What Jack did to her woman parts seemed scandalous, especially considering they weren't wed and were hiding among the trees. What if someone caught them?

She bit her lip as his finger probed her nether regions. Then a gentle breeze sent delicious shivers to her core. Was it Jack?

She lifted her head. Her billowing petticoats hid the attentions he provided. Another breeze caressed her folds. "Jack, what are you doing down there?"

He didn't answer, but delicious wetness seeped down her thighs. Intense tingles rose like a wave, carrying her along. She stifled the urge to cry out with pleasure. Covering her mouth in the folds of her sleeve, she muffled the cries his attentions drove from her.

She writhed and shook, until a crescendo sent her to a place she'd never been. Even when she'd lain with him in his hotel room, the feeling hadn't been this intense.

She sank into the leaves, panting. A warm lethargy nearly sent her into a swoon. "Oh, Jack," she breathed.

He emerged from beneath the white cotton, a huge grin on his face. "Liked that, did you?"

"Oh, yes."

He rose and patted down her clothing. "Now, we can rest and go over what we plan to do."

She sat up, her face heating at the recollection of his amorous attentions.

"You said you have the brooch and the photo?" He leaned on an elbow.

She nodded. "I just hope they send you back. I don't know what else will work."

"It's worth a try." He shrugged. "What else can we do?"

"But what if you can't take me with you?" She reached for his sleeve and ran her hand up to his shoulder. "What if I'm left here alone?"

He bit his lip. "I'll hold on tight, so if I go, you'll have to go too."

She shook her head. "I don't know, Jack. I'm afraid."

He settled his arm around her shoulder, drawing her into his strength and manly scent. "I won't let go. I swear."

****

By dusk, Jack could barely make out the framework of the house. Surely, the workmen had long since cleared out. He hoped they hadn't locked the house, but if they had, he could climb in one of the first floor windows and let Amanda in through the back door.

He glanced toward Amanda. In the dark, he couldn't tell if she was awake. She lay on her side, arms cradling her head.

He rolled toward her and prodded her arm, then leaned close to her face. Her breath quickened as his lips neared hers.

"If you're sleeping, angel, it's time to wake up. We have to go."

Her body stiffened. He tightened his arms around her, hoping she wouldn't scream.

"It's me, Jack," he whispered. "Don't be afraid."

She rolled toward him. "Jack, I can barely see you."

"We have to go. The workmen must be gone by now."

She nodded and with his assistance rose to her feet.

"Take my hand." He reached for her, then led her out of the half concealed shelter and into the open back yard. Glancing around, he listened intently for any sound out of the ordinary. The houses alongside Randolph's were too far away for anyone to hear or notice them in the deepening twilight.

At the steps leading up to the rear porch, he hesitated. "I want to be sure no one's still in there." He released Amanda's hand. "Stay here." Climbing the steps, he crept toward the window and peered inside. Although too dark to see the inner rooms, the absence of light convinced him no workers lingered. He stepped to the door.

A presence beside him sent his heart thudding, but the scent of Amanda eased his alarm.

He whirled around to face her. "I told you to stay put." His teeth clenched around the words.

"I was quiet," she protested. "So quiet, you didn't notice me."

He sighed. "Okay, let me see if this door is locked." He turned the knob, and the door opened inward. He stepped over the threshold, but hesitated, his pulse racing.

He turned toward Amanda. "Is this the kitchen we're entering?"

"I believe this door opens to the mud room. And that leads into the kitchen."

"Mud room," he repeated. "Of course, I'm thinking twenty-first century. In my time, the room we're going into was a sort of laundry room with a powder room."

"Powder room?" Amanda asked.

"Never mind. I just want to have a general idea of where I'm going in the dark."

"We should be able to find a lantern inside," Amanda reasoned. "We can use it to light our way upstairs."

He nodded. "We'll have to keep the light low, so the neighbors don't detect lights in here."

Grasping Amanda's hand, he led her through the doorway, then closed the door behind them. Adjusting his eyesight to the dimmer light inside proved difficult.

"Where do you think a lantern would be?" he asked.

"If the workmen were in the kitchen, likely in there."

He held his hand out in the direction of the inner wall. Squinting, he thought he glimpsed the outline of a door. Grasping the knob, he opened the door leading into the kitchen, his hearing straining for any sound in the house.

He led Amanda through the doorway, then shuffled through the large empty room. The side window allowed a bit of dim light, and he was able to make out the outline of what appeared to be an oil lamp in the center of the floor.

Amanda drew in a breath. "We need a match." Her hand slipped from his grasp.

"Be careful," he hissed.

"I've brought a small box in my bag."

"How resourceful." He smiled even though she

couldn't see his expression.

After a moment, the lamp ignited. "Here we are," Amanda said.

The soft glow illuminated her face. He reached for the lantern's handle and stepped toward the door, but hesitated. "I want to be sure no one's in the front rooms. You stay here with the lantern, while I take a look." He planted his hand on the kitchen door.

"But how will you see where you're going?" she protested.

"I'll use the light from the windows, and I know most of the layout of the house. I don't think it's changed much over the last couple hundred years."

She drew in a breath and crossed her arms over her chest. "Please be careful, Jack."

He nodded. "Be right back."

****

Amanda stood as still as she could manage while Jack checked the house. The last thing she wanted to do was alert anyone to their presence by the clicking of her heels over the bare floor.

She wrung her hands, her heart racing, ears straining for any sound. After what seemed like an hour, but was likely only a few minutes, the door opened to reveal Jack.

"All clear." He grasped the lantern's handle and motioned his head toward the door. "Follow me to the staircase, and we'll go back to the room."

She nodded, her mouth too dry to speak.

Following him up the staircase, she wondered if she'd done the right thing. But it was much too late to back out now.

He led her into the room where she'd first found

him over two weeks ago. Her life had changed so much since then.

He placed the lantern in the center of the room and motioned her to join him away from the windows. She glanced at the spot on the floor where she'd first found him sprawled out and hurt.

She took his hand. "What do we do now?"

He glanced at the bag fastened at her waist. "Give me the photo of you and the brooch."

She fished out the items and handed both to him.

He studied the photo. "I had this tucked into my pocket when I was hit with the beam." He opened his jacket and inserted the picture. "Like this." He patted the spot over his heart.

Amanda swallowed. "Jack, I'm a bit frightened, but I love you so. Please, don't leave me behind."

He shook his head. "Not if I have a choice in the matter."

She bowed her head, her hands clasped tight together.

He lifted her chin, so her gaze met his. "I don't ever want to leave you, Amanda." His lips found hers for a passion filled kiss. Thrilling tingles shot to her core.

Her arms tightened around him. She'd not allow him to slip through her fingers.

Pressing the brooch between them against both their hearts, Jack whispered, "Hold on tight."

She nodded.

After a few minutes of clinging together, she glanced around the room. "It isn't working, Jack. Nothing's changed."

His jaw tightened. "Something's wrong. We'll

have to figure out another plan. Your stepmother was so sure this room would do the trick."

A thump from downstairs set Amanda's heart racing. "Jack, someone's in the house."

Jack stilled against her as heavy footsteps mounted the stairs.

"What should we do?" Amanda lifted a fist and pressed it to her mouth.

"I'll put out the lamp." He extinguished the low glow. "Stay very still," he warned.

Amanda drew in a breath as something crashed down the hall. Footsteps echoed on the floor drawing closer.

"Jack," she murmured into his wool coat, "he's nearly here."

"Just stay with me, Amanda. I'll protect you."

She inhaled his comforting scent, but tensed as a shadowy figure holding a lantern stepped through the doorway. As he neared the center of the room, Amanda recognized the man.

"It's Randolph," she whispered.

Jack tensed.

"Who's there?" Randolph called, lifting the lantern. "Come out from hiding. You're trespassing."

Amanda yanked her hand from Jack's and stepped toward Randolph. She felt the brush of Jack's hand trying to pull her back, but didn't stop.

"It's me, Amanda."

"Amanda!" Randolph gasped. "Why the devil are you in my house in the dead of night?"

She drew herself up. "I could ask you the same question."

He sputtered. "It's my house. I can come here

anytime I like. You, on the other hand…" His gaze drifted to the corner where Jack stood. "Who's with you?"

Jack stepped toward them. "Jack Lawton." His gaze shifted to Amanda and he shook his head imperceptibly.

"You brought him here?" Randolph rounded on Amanda.

"No." Jack stepped between Amanda and Randolph. "I forced her to bring me here."

Amanda grasped Jack's shoulder from behind. "No, Jack, don't…"

"Ah, I see." Randolph leered. "A lovers' rendezvous, is it?"

"I forced her to come with me," Jack insisted. "She didn't want to."

Amanda didn't understand what Jack was doing. She only knew he wanted to protect her.

Randolph nodded. "I'm relieved I didn't take her to be my wife. You're nothing but a common strumpet, my dear."

Jack's face tightened. He stepped toward Randolph, so the two men stood nose to nose. "You'd better put the lantern down."

"Why?" Randolph asked.

When Jack didn't reply, Randolph set the lantern down and stepped back, an amused grin on his face.

"Do you plan to fight me for her?" He spread his arms wide. "You can have her? She's nothing but a whore lying with common workmen who spend their nights with their lips wrapped around a bottle of liquor."

Jack growled low in his throat and sprung at

Randolph. The stunned editor stepped back, but Jack's fist landed on his jaw, sending him to his knees.

Amanda's pulse thundered. "Jack, don't!" She stepped toward the brawling men.

"Amanda, stay back!" Jack commanded.

Randolph recovered and rolled away from Jack, grasping at an object on the floor. In the dim light, Amanda made out the shape of a wrench.

"Jack, look out!" she called.

Jack turned too late. Randolph clubbed him and Jack fell to the floor with a thud.

"What did you do?" Amanda raced forward and sank to her knees beside Jack. "You may have killed him!" She grasped Jack's face, trying to revive him. He slumped in her arms.

****

Jack woke with a monster headache.

Where the hell am I?

Voices murmured around him and the harsh glare of an electric light fixture hung over his bed. He frowned, trying to recall what had just happened. An image of Amanda in the glow of an oil lamp was replaced by Randolph. Randolph had hit him with something hard.

"Jack!" A woman's voice by his ear called out. "You're awake. Finally!"

He gazed up into the pale drawn face of his mother. He tried to speak but realized he had a tube inserted in his throat.

"Don't try to talk, Jack." She patted his arm. "You've been in a coma for weeks. They found you unconscious in that old house."

He blinked. He'd been in a coma the whole time?

Was any of what happened real? Was Amanda? He fought the urge to tear the tube from his throat to demand answers.

A woman dressed in scrubs rushed into the room. "Mrs. Lawton, did I hear you say he was awake?"

"Yes." His mother caught his gaze and nodded. "Thank God." She held his hand and gave a reassuring squeeze. "Everything's going to be all right now."

****

Two weeks later, Jack was still recovering from his blow to the head and subsequent coma. He had a hard time believing Amanda and everything that had happened to him in the nineteenth century had been a coma dream, but no other explanation made sense.

His mother gave him the jacket he'd been wearing the night of the accident, Amanda's photo still inside the pocket. His mother asked him who she was.

"I saw her photo hanging on the wall in the house and asked the new owner if I could have it."

"She's beautiful," his mother murmured.

"Yeah," he'd agreed.

Now, he was left to wonder at the vivid dream. He distinctly remembered Amanda's stepmother telling him the story of her return to the future and how she'd willed herself to come back to Amanda's father.

Could he do the same? Did he want to?

The memory of Amanda's scent and softness in his arms, as well as the time they'd spent in his hotel room and the grove at the back of the house, convinced him. If there was a way to go back, he had to give it a try.

But how? He still had the photo, but could he get back in the house?

The following day, he tucked the photo into his

inner jacket pocket and returned to the house. A string of yellow tape surrounded the structure and grounds.

His heart thudded as he realized it must be scheduled for demolition. If he couldn't get through now, the house would be gone forever.

He'd left a note at his apartment for his mother explaining where he'd gone. He couldn't leave her wondering, if he was able to actually pull this off. Glancing up and down the street, he ducked under the tape and scurried up to the front porch. He tried the door, and it wasn't locked. He didn't think it would be.

Easing himself inside, he closed the door behind him and strode to the foot of the stairs. He tested a stair to be sure it was stable, then slowly climbed. The interior of the house was cool and dusty. He hoped to hell demolition wasn't scheduled for today, but the lack of heavy equipment outside assured him he'd be safe, at least for the time being.

At the top of the staircase, he hesitated, then stepped down the hall toward the room where he'd traveled through time to Amanda. Would her photo be enough to send him back, or did he have to get smacked on the head with another beam? He surely hoped not.

Erin's story of her return gave him hope that desire alone would send him back to Amanda.

As he entered the room, he pulled out her photo. He held it up to a shaft of sunlight shining brightly through the bared window and glanced around the room. An ache knifed through his belly at the thought of this house being razed to the ground. No one would ever know who'd lived here. But if he couldn't make it back, his one wish was that Amanda didn't marry Randolph and found love with a better man. If he couldn't go back, though, he'd never know.

The empty space where Amanda's photo had been might have been occupied by another woman's photo. But if so, he wouldn't have the picture in his pocket. The paradoxes were agonizing. He had to get back to her. Now.

He knelt in the center of the floor and stared at the picture in his hands. "I love you, Amanda. I'm willing to give up my life here to spend my life with you." He kissed the photo. A shiver raced up his spine as the feel of her lips, her scent and softness enveloped him. She wasn't here, though, but in the past.

Closing his eyes, he went with the feeling. A wave of dizziness sent him reeling. He slumped to the floor.

****

"Jack!"

He gazed up into Amanda's beautiful face, her delicate brows drawn into a frown. Her arms cradled his shoulders as his head lay in her lap. She bent to kiss his forehead.

"I feared the devil killed you." Her gaze shifted across the room.

Jack glanced up. Randolph stood over him. In the dim light, the leer stretching across his face reminded Jack of a grinning skull. "Glad to see you're not dead, Lawton."

He reached out his hand. "Come, Amanda. This is no place for you. I'll see you home, then return for Mr. Lawton."

Amanda tightened her hold on Jack. "You will not, sir. I'll see Jack to my home so my stepmother can give him care."

"But his family…" Randolph protested.

"I'm his family now." Amanda eased Jack's head from her lap and rose. "We're going to marry."

Randolph's gaze narrowed. "Amanda, are you insane?"

She shook her head. "No, I am not. Please leave. I'll take care of him from now on."

Jack leaned on an elbow hoping to ease the spinning in his head.

Randolph glared at him, then Amanda. "If you do this, don't return to the office. You'll have no position there."

She bit her lip, then glanced down at Jack. "I don't care. I know where my future lies."

Randolph swore but stepped away and out the door. "Get him out of my house, and if either of you ever return, I'll have you brought up on trespassing charges." Jack listened for his footsteps descending the stairs, fearing he'd return to pummel him again or harm Amanda.

The sound of the front door opening and closing convinced him the man had left. He blew out the breath he'd been holding.

Amanda dropped to the floor beside Jack. "Can you walk?"

He gingerly tilted his head. "I think with your support, I'll make it back to my hotel room."

"Oh, no." Amanda shook her head. "You're coming to my house until I'm sure you've recovered."

"Guess I can't argue." He smiled. Amanda traced his lips with her finger, sending a tingle up his spine.

"I was afraid he'd killed you." She rose and helped him to stand. "I couldn't wake you."

He steadied himself as she held onto his arm. "It

was the damndest thing." His gaze captured hers. "I was home."

She gasped. "You were in the future?"

"Yeah. For nearly two weeks."

"But you were only out a few minutes." She gazed off into space.

"I was home, and all I could think of was getting back to you." He gathered her in his arms and kissed her lips. "I love you, Amanda. You brought me back here."

"But I wanted to go with *you*." She crossed her arms over her chest. "I want to live the modern life you keep telling me about."

He guided her to the door. "Let's go home and make wedding plans. Afterward, we'll try to figure out a way to get us both to the future. And if we can't..." He smiled. "...will it be so bad to live together here?"

Amanda grinned. "No, Jack, not at all."

A word about the author...

Susan Macatee sets her stories of romance during and just after the American Civil War. Her passion for this period in American history also extends to the paranormal. You'll find time travelers, ghosts, and vampires in the mix.

Her interest in the period stems from her years spent as a civilian Civil War reenactor, alongside her husband, who did the military side, with the 28th Pennsylvania Volunteer Regiment for about ten years.

She lives with her husband and sons, and the family dog, a boxer-mix named Chase.

She spends her free time cheering on her local baseball team, the Philadelphia Phillies, spending time with Chase and her husband, watching favorite old movies, and inhaling books.

Visit Susan's website for more
information about her books.
www.susanmacatee.com

Thank you for purchasing
this publication of The Wild Rose Press, Inc.
For other wonderful stories of romance,
please visit our on-line bookstore at
www.thewildrosepress.com.

For questions or more information
contact us at
info@thewildrosepress.com.

The Wild Rose Press, Inc.
www.thewildrosepress.com

To visit with authors of
The Wild Rose Press, Inc.
join our yahoo loop at
http://groups.yahoo.com/group/thewildrosepress/

www.ingramcontent.com/pod-product-compliance
Lightning Source LLC
Chambersburg PA
CBHW051243170626
46809CB00004B/1462